I KISSED AN EARL (AND I LIKE IT)

MERRY FARMER

I KISSED AN EARL (AND I LIKED IT)

Copyright ©2021 by Merry Farmer

This book is licensed for your personal enjoyment only. This book may not be re-sold or given away to other people. If you would like to share this book with another person, please purchase an additional copy for each recipient. If you're reading this book and did not purchase it, or it was not purchased for your use only, then please return to your digital retailer and purchase your own copy. Thank you for respecting the hard work of this author.

This book is a work of fiction. Names, characters, places, and incidents are products of the author's imagination or are used fictitiously. Any resemblance to actual events or locales or persons, living or dead, is entirely coincidental.

Cover design by Erin Dameron-Hill (the miracle-worker)

ASIN: B08RSNZ88C

Paperback ISBN: 9798700764377

Click here for a complete list of other works by Merry Farmer.

If you'd like to be the first to learn about when the next books in the series come out and more, please sign up for my newsletter here: http://eepurl.com/RQ-KX

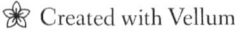 Created with Vellum

CHAPTER 1

DUNEGARD CASTLE, NEAR BALLYMENA, IRELAND – JULY, 1888

It was widely known throughout County Antrim, and Ireland in general, that the O'Shea family were wicked, scandalous, and unruly in every way imaginable. Particularly the ladies of the family. Young ladies with the surname O'Shea had been causing trouble and upsetting apple carts for generations. That went double for the untamed sisters of Lord Fergus O'Shea, Earl of Ballymena. All four of them. They were headstrong, opinionated, and a bit too enamored of the freedom their brother allowed them when he was away in England.

The sisters had taken up residence in a seaside cottage, where they had the audacity to live independently, in spite of being the daughters of an earl and ladies in their own right. They insisted on cooking their own meals, washing their own laundry, and keeping their own house. It was unspeakably scandalous. When asked, the eldest sister, Lady Shannon O'Shea, would argue that every woman, regardless of her rank, needed to master domestic skills, otherwise they would be completely at the mercy of others. And the O'Shea sisters had no intention of being at the mercy of anyone. Because one never knew which way the wind would blow when it came to the fortunes of the aristocracy, particularly the Ascendancy. So the sisters took their lives and their upkeep into their own hands, flouting convention, scandalizing their neighbors, and generally shocking both high and low with their wildly unusual views of the world and a woman's place in that.

But all that was about to change.

"It has come to my attention that I have been remiss in keeping my eye on you," Fergus said with a frown, addressing his sisters from his wheelchair in the family parlor of Dunegard Castle one summer morning. "And since I only have one eye left, it's even more important to use it wisely."

Marie O'Shea felt a wave of intense anger, in spite of her brother's jovial mood. She would have murdered the English dogs who attacked and nearly killed her brother several years ago, if the main perpetrator hadn't already been killed. Fergus was still as handsome and wily as the Devil, but he would forever be confined to a wheelchair now, in spite of the efforts of his friend and personal physician, Dr. Linus Townsend, to teach him to walk with crutches, and he'd lost an eye in the attack as well. Although he did look rather roguish wearing an eyepatch. His wife, Lady Henrietta, certainly thought so. She stood by Fergus's side now, grinning far too much for a woman whose husband was taking his sisters to task.

"Therefore," Fergus went on, "on the advice of the esteemed Lady Coyle here—" he gestured to the stoic, grey-haired lady standing on the other side of his wheelchair—a woman who saw it as her business to oversee the lives of every eligible young lady in the county, "—I have decided to evict you from your seaside home."

"What are you saying?" Shannon said, her expression turning stormy.

"You can't be serious," Chloe, the youngest sister, followed, crossing her arms.

"I knew something horrible would happen," Colleen, one of the middle sisters, along with Marie, said with a sigh.

"I should have put my foot down years ago," Fergus went on. His mouth twitched into a wry grin. "That's a bit of a challenge for me these days as well."

"Fergus, how can you joke at a time like this?" Marie said, stepping forward and planting her hands on her hips. "You've never had a problem with the four of us living at the cottage before this. We've always just gotten along, minding our own business, not hurting anyone."

Lady Coyle snorted. "Not hurting anyone?" she

repeated incredulously. "What about the emotional distress you have all caused the residents and shopkeepers of Ballymena?"

Marie blinked and stared at the woman. "We haven't done anything to any residents or shopkeepers."

"We do a lively trade with them," Shannon seconded her. "And more than a few of the pubs in town have appreciated our beer."

"And we will never reveal our secret recipe to a soul," Chloe said with a sparkle in her eyes.

Lady Coyle huffed as though the sisters had insulted her dignity and shook her head.

Fergus couldn't seem to stop grinning, but fought to school his expression all the same. "Surprisingly, several of the residents of Ballymena are unhappy with ladies of the local aristocracy making and selling beer. They aren't too pleased with the lot of you wading in the sea with your skirts tied up around your waists either."

"Or with the four of you dragging that telescope out in the middle of the night where men on their way home from the pub can see you," Henrietta added with a grin.

"What do those lecherous pigs care if we have an interest in astrology?" Chloe asked.

"Astronomy, dear," Shannon corrected her.

"Oh. Yes," Chloe said, looking sheepish, as though she had meant what she said. She was a Gemini, after all.

"If you ask me, there are quite a few people around here who should be minding their own business," Marie said, arching one eyebrow at Fergus. They'd done perfectly well with him away in England. As much as she loved her brother, part of her wished he were back there now.

"I don't mind if you all have minds of your own and use them," Fergus said with a shrug, "but as it turns out, others do." He shot a sideways glance to Lady Coyle. "Furthermore, it has been brought to my attention that the lot of you are perilously close to being on the shelf. Shannon, you're just shy of thirty."

Shannon opened her mouth to protest, but before she could say anything, Lady Coyle hissed, "It's unconscionable that none of the four of you are married, and at your ages. As I have explained to your brother, there are more than enough men of suitable title and fortune eager to marry the sisters of an earl, no matter how *lively* they are. The time has come for all of you to wed."

The sisters gaped and snorted in offense, shaking their heads and huffing.

"I don't object to marriage," Marie said, narrowing her eyes at her brother. "I'd rather like the excuse to have a man in my bed."

Lady Coyle groaned and pinched the bridge of her nose. Marie's sisters laughed.

"Come to think of it, you're right there," Colleen said.

"I wouldn't mind a strapping, virile man at all," Shannon agreed.

"As long as he's a Leo," Chloe added. "Or Aquarius. I suppose Aries would do."

"Good. It's settled, then," Fergus said, a little too

forcefully, as though the sisters had just walked blissfully into a trap. "Pack up your things and bring them back to the castle immediately. I'll have all your old bedrooms prepared for you."

"Now hold on just a moment," Colleen led the protests.

"This isn't fair," Marie huffed.

"We're perfectly fine at the cottage," Shannon said.

Fergus held up his hands against the onslaught of protest. "Enough of that, now, ladies," he said, silencing them all. By his side, Henrietta had to hide her mouth in her hand to stifle her laughter. Marie bristled at the gesture, but Fergus went on before she could say anything. "I'm determined to marry you four hellions off," he said. "And to do that, even though it might kill me, I'm going to have to host gatherings and invite suitable men from respectable families to do things like dine with us."

"Ugh." Chloe grimaced. "I despise the word 'respectable'."

"Yes, I can imagine you do," Lady Coyle said in a flat voice.

Fergus sent her a weary look, then focused on his sisters once more. "You'll all move back to the castle. We'll entertain and do all the things an earl and his family should do." Marie and the others groaned in protest. "But," Fergus went on, holding up a hand, "because I know how much of a trial this is for you, I have a peace offering."

"What sort of a peace offering?" Shannon asked, one brow raised.

"Michael," Fergus called toward the hallway, summoning his head footman.

Michael appeared in the doorway a moment later, as if he'd been waiting around the corner, listening for his cue in a stage production. He wasn't alone when he entered the room, though, and he wasn't empty-handed. Marie gasped and pressed a hand to her stomach as Michael and the other footman, Sean, entered the room, each of them wheeling two bicycles with them.

"Dear God above, those aren't what I think they are," Colleen said, leaping toward the footmen.

"Bicycles," Chloe squealed, following her. Her expression lit to absolute joy. She immediately snatched one of the newfangled contraptions from Michael and gazed at it, enraptured. "Oh! These are the new safety bicycles Mr. Starley invented. I've been reading about them everywhere. They're becoming all the rage in smart circles."

"Oh, good heavens," Lady Coyle groaned as though she might faint. "Lord O'Shea, what have you done?"

Marie didn't wait around for the answer. She and Shannon rushed toward Sean, taking the last two bicycles from him. Marie's heart raced as she pored over the amazing invention. She'd played with bicycles where one wheel was enormous and the other was small, but both wheels of the machines Fergus had purchased were the same size. They were part of the new design that involved a chain to turn the wheels. The bicycle in her hands was clearly meant for a woman to use, as the chain had a metal covering to prevent skirts from catching in the mechanism.

"It's the most beautiful thing I've ever seen," she gasped, running her hand over the leather seat.

"It's clearly a bribe," Shannon said, though she couldn't pull her eyes off her bicycle.

"You are correct, dear sister," Fergus said. "I am giving each of you one of these machines in exchange for your cooperation in moving back into the castle and marrying men whom I deem suitable."

"You're not going to pick them out for us, are you?" Colleen said, snapping her head up and narrowing her eyes.

"Only if you make it necessary," Fergus said. "Otherwise, I'm more than willing to take suggestions."

Marie snorted at that, but her heart was still too full of her new plaything to pay much mind to her brother. She wondered how difficult bicycles were to ride. She'd seen illustrations, read instructions, and figured she'd do all right, but there was only one way to tell.

"I want to take it for a ride right this very moment," she said, glancing to her sisters.

"So do I," Chloe gasped with equal excitement.

"Go right ahead," Fergus said. "Provided you ride those things down to the cottage to pack your belongings and have them sent back to the castle."

The sisters stopped perusing their bicycles and

I KISSED AN EARL (AND I LIKE IT)

snapped straight. Marie had been right to sense a trap earlier. That trap had closed around her as certainly as if she were a rodent who had just had its neck snapped.

"Do we have an agreement?" Fergus asked. "Those bicycles in exchange for your residence at the castle?"

The sisters exchanged looks. Marie knew immediately they'd all been had. The problem was, Fergus had chosen exactly the right bait for his trap.

"All right," Marie answered first. "You win this time, dear brother. I agree to move back into the castle for the purpose of marrying me off. As long as whatever man you find who might be willing to marry me accepts Lucifer along with my hand."

"Lucifer?" Henrietta asked, still having a difficult time not laughing.

Marie smiled at her bicycle. "That's what I'm going to call it."

Her sisters laughed. Lady Coyle looked as though she might faint.

"Let's take them outside and see if we can ride them," Shannon said, wheeling her bicycle toward the door.

"Yes, I'm determined to master this," Colleen agreed and followed her.

They all turned their bicycles around and pushed them toward the hall. Before leaving, Marie called over her shoulder, "Thank you, Fergus. You're going to regret this."

"Don't you mean I'm *not* going to regret this?" Fergus asked.

9

Marie laughed mischievously. "No, you will absolutely regret it."

Judging by the sound Lady Coyle made as the sisters left, taking their bicycles out to the front drive, she believed Fergus had made an unforgivably grave mistake.

It was the perfect day to learn how to ride a bicycle. As soon as the four of them reached the front drive, they leapt into the task. The bicycles were clearly designed for ladies with skirts, though perhaps not as many petticoats as they all wore. Marie solved that problem by hitching up her skirt and removing the frilly petticoat she'd donned when the four of them were called to their audience with Fergus. She managed to make poor Sean blanch in the process. But immediately she discovered that it was far easier to mount and peddle a bicycle without a copious amount of fabric around her legs.

"It's not as difficult as I thought it would be," she called to her sisters as she propelled herself forward, making a large circuit of the front drive. "As long as you can keep your balance, the faster you go, the easier it is."

"I've heard that about a few other things," Shannon said with a wicked wink, peddling her bicycle shakily.

The others were getting the hang of things, but slowly. Chloe didn't seem comfortable sitting on the seat. Shannon stopped what she was doing to examine the bicycle to see if there was a way to make the seat lower. Colleen looked as though she could balance, but she wasn't moving fast enough, and her bicycle kept careening to the side. By contrast, the more Marie rode around in the circle of the drive, the more confident she felt.

"Well, I'm off," she said with a spritely air as she made a final loop around the drive. "I'll see you lot back at the cottage."

If her sisters protested over the way she broke free and peddled away from the castle, Marie didn't hear them. She shot down the long stretch of the drive that led to the front gate and the road, then picked up speed, flying on down the slight incline of the road.

It felt very much like flying as well, or what she imagined flying might be like. The wind whipped through her hair, pulling ginger strands out of the careless style she'd pushed it into earlier. She should have been wearing a hat, but she hadn't bothered to fetch hers before rushing outside with her bicycle, and she was glad for it. There was something magical about speeding along the road, sunlight glowing down on her, the green of the landscape around her meeting the blue of the summer sky. She could smell grass, wildflowers, and the salt of the sea. Sunlight baked her, and the more she peddled, the warmer she became. Her heart thundered against her ribs with the effort of riding, but she loved every moment of it. If Fergus had given them the bicycles as a peace offering for taking away their freedom, he had the bad end of the bargain. Marie had never felt so free in her life.

The feeling lasted all the way until she reached the cliffs and sheltered coves of the sea. That was when she realized that, as beautiful as the world was and as joy-filled as her heart felt, stopping a bicycle was more of a challenge than starting one.

"Oh, dear," she muttered to herself as she stiffened, staring down at the bicycle under her and wondering if there were some sort of braking mechanism. She should have checked before peddling into high speed. The handlebar seemed to have something of a brake on it, but she was too afraid of crashing to squeeze it with any enthusiasm.

In the end, she did the only thing she could think to do. She steered off the road toward a stretch of sandy beach. At the very least, the sand would cushion her fall if she ended up flying over the handlebars in her efforts to stop.

The grass dividing the road from the cove went a long way to slow the bicycle, and by the time she rolled out onto the sand, she'd lost enough speed to risk squeezing what she thought was a handbrake. Sure enough, the bicycle stopped completely. Marie let out a yelp as she jerked forward, then crumpled to the side as she lost her balance. She and the bicycle fell in a tumble of metal and skirts.

"Are you all right?" a rich, tenor voice called from the direction of the water.

Marie yelped again, embarrassed to have been caught crashing, and glanced around furtively. She saw no one close by on the sandy beach or near the small cliff that sheltered half of the beach from the road. The road was

I KISSED AN EARL (AND I LIKE IT)

clearly empty, which meant the voice could only be coming from the water itself.

Sure enough, as she scrambled into a crouch, ready to stand, she spotted a man, just over waist-deep in the sea. He must have been kneeling, as he wasn't far out enough for the water to be that deep. His bare chest glistened in the sunlight, highlighting lean, toned muscles and whorls of dark hair that stuck damply to his skin. He had dark, curly hair on his head to match, dancing eyes, and a broad smile with surprisingly straight, white teeth. The sight of him thrilled Marie more than the bicycle.

She stood straight as quickly as she could, brushing sand from her skirt. "I am quite all right," she said, her own smile growing. "Just taking Lucifer for a turn about the countryside."

"I take it Lucifer is your bicycle," he said, his grin more mischievous than ever.

"Not that it's anything to you, but yes," she said, crossing her arms and striking a bold pose as she ogled his bare chest. The man knelt there in the water, fine as you please, not seeming to care that she was taking in the full sight of him.

"Oh, I see." His smile widened. "How interesting for a woman to name a bicycle after a fallen angel."

"It takes one to know one," Marie said, unable to tear her eyes away from him.

He laughed. The sound was luxurious and exciting. It did things to her insides. Things that were exacerbated by the way the waves washed in and out around the man's waist, giving her hints of far more than she should be looking at now and then. The bounder wasn't wearing drawers.

"And you're certain you're not injured in any way?" he asked, continuing to tease her with his eyes.

"Perfectly uninjured in every way," she told him. "And yourself?"

"Oh, I'm grand," he said, inching forward a bit and looking as though he might stand. "I was worried that you might have hit your head, you see."

"My head?" Marie blinked, lowering her arms.

"Seeing as you seem unable to gather your wits about you or look away, like a well-bred young lady should."

There was something tantalizing and challenging about his comment. Whether he was genuinely hinting for her to give him a moment of modesty so he could wade out of the water to fetch his clothes—which she now saw sitting in a pile farther down the beach—or daring her to keep looking, she couldn't quite tell. So she chose to keep looking.

"My head is right as rain," she said, then nodded to the parts of him below the water. "Is yours?" She said a quick prayer of thanks for all the rough language she'd learned through selling their beer to the local pubs.

"Perhaps you should judge for yourself," he said.

And then he did the wildest and most shocking thing Marie had ever witnessed in her life. He stood up.

Water cascaded down his perfect form, sluicing over fine, strong hips and thighs, highlighting his narrow waist, and making him glisten like a mythical creature. But that was nothing to the sight of the dark hair around his groin and the bold, masculine shape of his balls and penis. The water must have been cold enough that he wasn't in any sort of an aroused state, but Marie hardly cared. There it was, bold as you please, kissed by sunlight, an impressive cock. The man had the audacity to rest his hands on his hips and grin like a fool as she drank in the sight of him, either not caring that he was on full display for her or reveling in it. Indeed, when she finally managed to get her eyes to snap up to meet his face, the man looked downright proud of himself for standing there as God made him. And God had made him well.

"It would appear that we have a bit of a dilemma on our hands," he said, his voice lowering to a sultry timbre.

Marie almost didn't hear him. She was too busy staring. Her day had just turned far more interesting than she'd bargained for. "What dilemma is that?" she asked, pretending nothing was amiss, even though she could feel her face heating.

"We haven't been properly introduced," the man said, obviously well-mannered and polite. Except for the whole shameless nudity thing.

He started toward the beach, veering off as though he intended to fetch his clothes. Marie wasn't having any of that, though. She abandoned Lucifer in an instant and darted across the sand, intent on reaching his clothing before he did.

CHAPTER 2

*C*hristian's heart shot to his throat—or perhaps an organ slightly lower—as Lady Marie O'Shea dashed toward his clothes on the shore. He knew who she was, of course. By sight and by reputation. He wasn't certain whether she recognized him. He'd been away at university and then on a tour of the continent, after all, and had only just returned home a few months earlier. And besides, a lady like Marie O'Shea would have no reason to know who the younger son of an earl of middling importance was.

She was after his clothes. That was all that mattered. He picked up his pace, splashing through the shallows toward the beach, cock swinging freely, trying to decide whether he hoped he reached his clothes before her or not. He wasn't in the habit of lying to himself, and frankly, he appreciated the look of bold interest that Lady Marie had given him. Appreciated it and more. If not for the cold water, he might have given her more to look at. There was still a danger of embarrassment on that front, but Christian didn't care. He was who he was, and he loved that about himself.

"Ha!" Marie shouted as she pounced on his clothes. She gathered them into her arms, then wheeled back as if she would hold them hostage indefinitely. "Now you're in a pinch."

Christian splashed his way out of the water and across the beach to stand several yards in front of her, hands on his hips, cock hanging. He paused to catch his breath and grinned at her, then shook his head. "And what sort of a pinch is that?" he asked.

She didn't even try to hide the fact that she was staring at him, so he didn't hide how much he liked it. It certainly wasn't the first time he'd engaged in conversation while swinging free. Although there was generally a great deal more alcohol involved, and he hadn't been in that position since Italy.

Marie swallowed hard, then snapped her eyes up to meet his again as she hugged his clothes. For a moment, she wore a startled look. Then she burst into a sheepish laugh. "Do you know, I forgot completely what I was going to say."

"Yes, I have that effect on people," he said with a wink.

"Do you, now?" she asked, arching one eyebrow.

"I think it's because of my blistering wit and magnificent intelligence." He shifted his weight slightly, standing as though they were meeting in a ballroom and he was fully clothed.

Her lips twitched and her eyes danced with humor. "I suppose you're exactly the sort of lad people like to invite to their parties, then?"

"That goes without saying." Christian shrugged. Her gaze dropped to his groin again. He knew full well she was a lady, but that didn't cool his urge to handle himself to see how she reacted. He refrained, of course. He might not have been anyone destined for greatness—his position in the family didn't even warrant use of the prefix "Lord" —but his father was an earl. A little decorum with a member of his own class was necessary.

But not enough to make any sort of move to retrieve his clothes from her.

"You still haven't introduced yourself," she reminded him in a hoarse voice a moment later, meeting his eyes again.

"I'm surprised you didn't remember me on sight," he said, taking a step forward. Her eyes widened and she snuck another look at his willy. "Christian Darrow?" he said, forming it as a question to see if the name would jog her memory. "Lord Kilrea's errant and prodigal younger son."

Marie's mouth dropped open—which was entirely distracting, since she was still staring at his cock and the sight of her pink lips parted that way threatened to give her more than she bargained for to look at—and she gasped in recognition. "Aren't you in Spain or some such?" she asked, gaze meeting his again at last.

"Yes," he answered, trying not to laugh. "That's where we are at present, is it not?"

Marie snapped her mouth shut and sent him a flat look.

"I must have gone for a longer swim than I thought and washed up on this shore instead of the one near Bilbao." He winked for good measure.

"Well, then, you won't be needing these." She tossed her armful of his clothes behind her. "You can just swim back to Spain and fetch the clothes you left there."

"I could." He shrugged. "But who needs clothes on a fine, warm day like this. I trust you're warming up yourself, Lady Marie?"

His pointed teasing didn't have quite the effect he'd hoped for. Any other fine lady whose acquaintance he'd ever made would be fainting with embarrassment at the sight of him. All of him. Part of him wanted to see how far he could push things to make Lady Marie faint as well. Except that if she hadn't already, if she wasn't falling all over herself in an effort not to stare at his naked body, he doubted there was anything short of vulgarity that he could do to put her off.

Not that he wanted to put her off. Quite the opposite.

God, he liked her.

After a heavy pause, she blinked and glanced up again. "You know who I am?" she asked.

"All of Ireland knows who you are, Lady Marie O'Shea," he said, adding a wink.

"Thank God," she said in a seemingly relieved voice.

Christian wondered if she truly was relieved or if he'd finally embarrassed her by mentioning her reputation. Her face was a little too pink, and her eyes sparkled a bit too much. Whether she was letting on or not, he'd unnerved her at least a little bit. Which was grand, as far as he was concerned.

Her gaze started to drop again, but she cleared her throat and crossed her arms. "So you're back in Ireland, then, Mr. Christian Darrow."

"I am," Christian said with a nod, unable to resist adding, "In the flesh." He peeked down at himself.

Marie burst into a snort that she had to hide with one hand to her mouth. "And what fine flesh it is too," she added, giggling as she did.

That was it. Christian was charmed beyond reason. He'd taken a shine to women on site in the past, as they had to him, but the instant draw he felt toward Lady Marie went beyond any of those trifling feelings. Any woman who could endure his naked company with both appreciation and a snort of laughter was the sort of woman he wanted to be friends with. Or more. In spite of the fact that his father would chastise him for having no decorum or discretion. Perhaps because of it. His bloody father had never understood the way he enjoyed life. If his father had had his way, every man on earth would be boring and stolid and—

And the last thing he wanted to think about when faced with a beautiful nymph like Lady Marie was his failure to live up to his father's expectations.

"What brings you to this bit of beach that I thought was secluded enough for a dip in the middle of the afternoon?" he asked, shifting his weight but continuing to pretend there was nothing unusual about him having the conversation naked.

"My brother has just given me a bicycle," she explained.

"Lucifer," he said, proving he remembered the name.

"And I was exploring," she finished.

"I bet you were," he said, one eyebrow flickering.

She laughed out loud, and perhaps would have said more if a hint of movement from beyond the beach hadn't distracted them both. They turned to find an old woman—likely from one of the nearby villages—strolling along the road. She had a basket over one shoulder and was singing to herself.

"Quick," Christian hissed, dropping to his knees on the sand. "When she sees us, pretend I've just washed up on the shore."

"What do you—you can't just—how do you expect—" Marie issued her flurry of protests, but giggled even harder as he flopped to his stomach, arms spread, feigning death. "Oh, you are a corker, aren't you," she mumbled, dropping to her knees beside him.

A moment later, the old woman's singing stopped and turned into an alarmed shout.

"Help, oh, help!" Marie called out to her—a little overdramatic, but still admirable in her enthusiasm.

Christian jolted as Marie's hands spread across his shoulders and she leaned closer to him. He could smell the faint scent of flowers and soap wafting from her in a combination he'd never known before. The heat of her body close to his was as delightful as the sun. He was glad he'd positioned himself face-down in the sand, because the effects of the cold water were wearing off fast as blood rushed to his cock.

"Please help me," Marie called out, slightly quieter as the old woman's footsteps swished across the sand.

"Oh! Oh, dear! Who is that?" the woman croaked, perhaps a little more alarmed than their impromptu prank should have made her.

"He washed in from the sea," Marie said, just enough of a note of humor in her voice to hint that she sensed their joke could go too far as well.

"From the sea, you say?" the old woman asked.

"I was riding my bicycle, and I stopped to dip my toes in the water," Marie told her, one hand still on his back as she twisted, presumably toward the woman. Christian had his eyes closed, so he could only guess what Marie looked like. "I was sitting here on the beach, enjoying my day and watching what I thought was a magnificent seal playing in the surf. Then, all of a sudden, I realized it wasn't a seal at all. Before I knew it, the tide pushed him in, and he swept up onto the shore like this."

She ran a hand down his spine, briefly caressing his

backside. It was all Christian could do to lie still as his cock jumped and pressed uncomfortably into the sand. Perhaps attempting to out-cheek Lady Marie O'Shea wasn't such a bright idea after all. He had no idea how he would get out of the predicament he'd found himself in with his dignity intact.

"Heavens above, child," the old woman gasped. "You must get away from him at once."

"But I cannot," Marie protested dramatically. "I feel drawn to him, captivated. Almost as though a spell were at work."

Christian caught himself hoping that she bloody well did feel captivated by him. That thought threatened to spoil his composure completely. He was supposed to be passed out, after all. He wanted to grin from ear to ear and learn more about Marie. Any woman who could play along with a prank moments after meeting him when he was as naked as the day he was born, was a woman he desperately needed in his life.

"Drawn, you say?" For a moment, the old woman sounded curious. Then she sucked in a hard breath. "Bless us all and saint's preserve us," she gasped. "Get away from the creature, woman. He'll capture you and drag you back into the sea for certain."

"But he needs my help," Marie sighed, both hands caressing his back now.

If Christian were a betting man, he would have said Marie was manhandling him with the specific intent of arousing him. Where in the bloody hell had a young lady from an aristocratic family got it in her mind to torture a man like him?

"He's a *selkie*, girl," the old woman scolded Marie.

"A...a what?" Marie asked with false innocence.

"A seal that's taken human form," the woman explained. Judging by the way Marie inched suddenly away from him, Christian assumed the old woman had grabbed her arm and attempted to pull her away. "He'll steal you away into the sea, girl," the old woman went on. "He'll seduce you away from all that is good and holy, and that will be the end of you."

"I've never been seduced away from all that is good and holy," Marie said, almost as though she liked the idea. She was a woman who had named her bicycle Lucifer, after all.

"Hurry, child, hurry," the old woman urged her. The shuffling of her feet across the sand hinted to Christian that she was trying to get away. "Get away before it's too late."

"But he's so...alluring." Marie returned to stroking his back. She might as well be stroking his prick for the reaction he had to her touch. Perhaps joking with the old woman had been a bad idea after all. "He's so warm and magnificent," Marie went on. She spread one hand across his backside and gave his cheek a squeeze.

Christian jerked and made a strangled noise. "Are you trying to get the two of us in a muddle?" he muttered, sand sticking to his lips as he did.

Marie lowered her voice to a vixen's purr near his ear.

"Are you going to seduce me and drag me back into the sea?"

It was too much. Christian burst into laughter, opening his eyes and peeking up at Marie. He scanned the beach quickly for the old woman. The poor dear was racing away on the road, her back to him and Marie. That was enough to convince him it was safe to get up—which he started to do, but stopped abruptly when he got as far as propping himself on his elbows. Rising any farther would be out of the question. He was already fully risen.

Marie inched back, a wicked grin tugging at the corners of her mouth, and sat with her hand bracing behind her. "I suppose it's safe for you to go get your clothes now," she said, nodding to his pile of clothes several yards away.

"Not at the moment," he said with a sheepish laugh, face heating.

"Why not?" Marie glanced over her shoulder at the old woman's retreating form. "She isn't looking back this way, you know." She faced forward again, staring saucily at him and biting her lip.

Christian laughed. "You're the daughter of an earl, aren't you?" he asked.

"I am." Marie nodded. "Though it would be more accurate these days to say I'm the sister of an earl, since dear Papa passed many years ago."

"The details are irrelevant," Christian said, doing his best to appear completely at ease as his erection pressed into the sand. "Aren't you too well-born and proper to have the sort of knowledge that would prompt you to know why I'm not getting up?"

Marie laughed aloud. "You have been away too long." She shifted to lean forward, splaying across the sand in a similar pose to the one he was stuck in, her face coming within inches of his. "Don't you know that the Wicked O'Shea Sisters are the scourge of County Antrim?"

"Yes, well, I had heard you lot were a bit unruly," Christian said in as off-hand a manner as he could manage.

"Unruly hardly begins to describe it," Marie said, lowering her voice.

It suddenly occurred to Christian that sand did not mix well with a raging erection. He feigned utter composure, though, determined to ignore the irritation that wasn't helping his body settle. "If this is how you comport yourself with men you've only just met, I'm astounded that your brother hasn't locked all of you away in a convent."

"We're not Catholic," Marie said, her voice more and more of a purr as she inched closer to him. She might not have had his cock to stare at anymore, but that didn't stop her from gazing hungrily at his lips.

Which did nothing at all for his chances of standing up anytime soon. "If not a convent, then an asylum," he said, matching her sultry tone. God, but he wanted to kiss her. He wanted to do more than that, if he were honest. And he wasn't the sort to go around debauching aristocratic ladies on beaches. He'd caroused his way through

I KISSED AN EARL (AND I LIKE IT)

university, enjoyed himself thoroughly in Europe, but it took coming home to Ireland for him to feel truly in over his head in matters of desire.

"My dear brother would have to catch me before he could put me in an asylum," Marie went on, her lips only a breath away from his. "And poor Fergus has just made the fatal error of giving me the means to peddle away from him whenever I want." Her eyes flashed as they met his. "What kind of mischief do you suppose I might get into with that sort of freedom?" she asked.

"I cannot imagine," Christian said, pulsing with lust and feeling startlingly on the back foot for a change.

"Fortunately," Marie went on, her breath tickling his lips and his heart pounding, "I have never been the sort to have a hard time deciding on things. I tend to know what I want the moment I see it."

"Oh?" Blast him, but his voice shook on the single-syllable word.

"And I've seen it, Christian Darrow," she continued, arching one amorous eyebrow, her full lips forming a wicked grin. "I've seen it all."

He started to laugh, but she stopped the sound by leaning toward him and kissing him soundly. She kissed him. Not that he wouldn't have kissed her just as hard himself, if he'd had the jump on her. He wasn't about to let her have the upper hand for long, though. Regardless of his state of arousal, he pushed himself up until he could reach for her and drag her into his arms. It was pure and utter madness. They'd barely met, but since when had formalities or time stood in the way of the absolute pleasure of kissing a woman who was game?

And Marie was most certainly ready for it. She slid her sandy arms over his shoulders and sighed deep in her throat as he devoured her mouth with giddy pleasure. It was wrong, mad, and the single most exciting thing he'd ever done. But most of all, kissing Marie, parting her lips so that his tongue could dance against hers, filled him with joy like nothing ever had before. One taste and he had the wild feeling that he would never be able to get enough of her. Not even if—

"Good God in heaven above, what is the meaning of this?"

The booming shout came from closer to the road. The spell that had been cast over Christian and Marie seemed to evaporate with a snap as the imposing form of Lady Coyle glared down at them.

"L-lady Coyle," Christian stammered. He started to shift then realized there was no possible way he could untangle himself from Marie and her conveniently concealing skirts without causing them all a great deal more embarrassment than they were already suffering under.

"Oh, dear," Marie gulped.

She started to move as well. She stood carefully, holding her skirts out to the sides as an effective curtain that allowed Christian to stand up as well. If only he wasn't half as *upstanding* as he obviously was. Although that situation was well on its way to deflating.

I KISSED AN EARL (AND I LIKE IT)

"I have never been so outraged in all my life," Lady Coyle raged at the two of them, face splotched red. "I thought that I had seen the very nadir of behavior from you O'Shea girls, but this?" Lady Coyle squeaked.

"I'm terribly sorry, Lady Coyle," Marie said, laughing nervously. "It was a joke that got a bit out of hand, you see."

"A joke?" That made Lady Coyle squeal even louder. "You think this sort of gross impropriety is a *joke*?"

"It was only meant as a jest," Christian said, backing Marie up and scrambling for a way to make the situation better.

He came up blank. Worse still, Lady Coyle's outrage only seemed to grow as she stared at the awkward pair he and Marie made.

"That is it," Lady Coyle hissed. "Lady Marie, come here at once. Although I have only just come from there, I am taking you back to your brother at once." She held out her hand and snapped her fingers for Marie to get moving.

"Um, er...." Marie hesitated, glancing over her shoulder at Christian's sand-covered body.

"At once," Lady Coyle shouted. "We will avert our eyes so that Mr. Darrow may make himself presentable."

"I doubt that's going to happen anytime soon," Christian muttered against Marie's ear.

Marie snorted into laughter, but that only enraged Lady Coyle.

"Lady Marie, if you do not get away from that man

and accompany me back to your brother's house this instant, I will make certain that not a single respectable house in all of Ireland will accept you, not a single person will claim to know you, and your brother will be forced to send you to the very darkest asylum in Peru."

"You see?" Christian murmured. "I told you it would be an asylum."

"Ssh," Marie hushed him, clearly having a hard time suppressing a giggle. "I'm coming, Lady Coyle. And I am ready to accept whatever punishment you and Fergus see fit to dole out." She stepped away from Christian, starting toward her bicycle. A few yards away, she glanced over her shoulder, giving Christian's sandy body a once-over. "It was worth it," she said with the most wicked grin Christian had ever seen.

Lady Coyle fussed, Marie fetched her bicycle, and the two of them walked off as Christian dashed out into the sea again to wash the sand off his body. His mind reeled from the wild turn his morning had taken. He let the cold water do its work, shriveling his balls almost as effectively as Lady Coyle had. He wouldn't be able to get Marie out of his blood any time soon, though. One kiss, and he was gone. Suddenly, he was bloody glad he'd come home after all his adventures.

CHAPTER 3

"Never, in all my days, have I ever so much as *heard* of anything as wicked and shameful as what you've done," Fergus shouted at Marie the next morning. "And in broad daylight, by the side of the main road as well. It's unconscionable. It's reckless. It's...."

Fergus dissolved into red-faced trembling, apparently unable to find a word bad enough to hurl at Marie.

Henrietta had to rest a hand on his shoulder to settle him. "Calm yourself, darling," she spoke softly. "Linus is in England, and the nearest physician would take hours to get here. I won't have you giving yourself apoplexy over a foolish girl."

Marie sank into herself at the steadily-delivered scolding from Henrietta. All the shouting and gesticulating that Fergus could summon up wasn't half as devastating as the quiet barb and disapproving look from Lady Henrietta. Marie grasped her hands in front of her, peeking to the side, where her three sisters stood, watching her have her head ripped off for her indiscretions with Christian the day before.

"It's not as though anything actually happened," she defended herself with as much backbone as she dared, which wasn't much.

Fergus, who was trying to breathe evenly, nearly leapt out of his wheelchair. "Not as though anything happened?" For a moment, Marie was afraid his good eye would pop right out of its socket. "You were seen canoodling with Lord Kilrea's son on the beach, *and the son in question was naked.*"

Marie flinched as he shouted the last part of the accusation so loudly she feared he would damage his voice. She wanted to grin and smirk over her memory of Christian's glorious form. The man had nothing to be ashamed of, and indeed, she wasn't ashamed of a single thing. In spite of every rule of propriety that had ever been thrown in her face and her brother's rage over the whole thing, she rather admired Christian for his fearlessness. And for his stunning form.

"Well-bred ladies do *not* converse with naked gentlemen on beaches," Fergus shouted on. "I don't know where you got it in your head to behave so wickedly. You shouldn't even know about such things. The sight of a man's body should make you faint in terror at the very least."

Marie let out a heavy sigh and rolled her eyes. "Really, Fergus. This is not the Middle Ages. We're almost in the twentieth century. Women are not ignorant ninnies anymore who need table legs covered for fear of—"

"You are my sister, and you have a level of respectability to maintain because of it," Fergus silenced her.

"But, Fergus—" Marie snapped her mouth shut and lowered her head slightly when it looked as though her brother might regain every bit of his power of movement through sheer willpower for the express purpose of lunging at her to wring her neck.

"How could you possibly think in a thousand years that even one moment of what you did yesterday was anything close to appropriate?" Fergus went on. One of Marie's sisters made a sound, and Fergus jerked to glare at them. "And don't think the rest of you are safe from the same sort of censure." He pointed at each of them in turn. "You're all as bad as the next. I should have heeded the letters Lady Coyle has been sending me for years and come home to dispose of you all much sooner."

Marie had the uncomfortable feeling that by "dispose" her brother meant in shallow, unmarked graves and not through matrimony.

"Mr. Darrow was bathing in the ocean." Marie tried one last effort to diffuse the situation. "He was the one who stood up and walked toward me on the beach."

"And you should have turned and fled," Fergus roared, not even slightly appeased, "not fallen into conversation with the man while all his bits were hanging."

It took a supreme effort of will for Marie not to snort at the remembered image of those hanging bits. Or the dark thatch of curls that surrounded them, or the firm plane of Christian's stomach, his strong muscles, or his sun-kissed skin glittering with saltwater as he—

"So help me God, Marie, if that smirk is an indication of you remembering what you saw, I will lock you away in the tiniest broom closet this castle has and keep you there until you're old and shriveled," Fergus growled.

"I was not imagining anything," Marie lied, her face heating.

"I don't believe you for a moment," Fergus said. "I knew you were a saucy strumpet, but I had no idea you would go this far to fling the laws of man and of nature out the window."

"I did no such thing," Marie argued with sudden force. She planted her fists on her hips and took a step toward her brother. "I was polite to Mr. Darrow, and yes, we had a bit of fun that some people would see as inappropriate. But it's not as though I stripped my own clothes off and flung myself at him." Though she had to admit that patting his bum while pretending he was a seklie might have crossed a line or two. It was such a nice bum, though—firm and warm and the perfect handful. She wouldn't have minded exploring much more of Christian's exquisite body. For scientific purposes, of course.

Fergus wasn't amused by her argument. "You're only lucky that his cousin, John, back in England is a close friend of mine. Otherwise, I would challenge the lecherous blackguard to pistols at dawn."

"Fergus." Marie rolled her eyes and crossed her arms. "No one duels anymore, and even if they did, you're in no —" She stopped herself short at the flash of hurt in her brother's eyes. The attack had happened years ago, but no one in the family had truly talked about it since then. A lump formed in Marie's throat at the sudden knowledge of what her brother had lost and how much it still hurt him.

She cleared her throat and went on while Fergus was still stung. "I like Mr. Darrow. He's jolly and free. I could see right away that he's a man who knows how to have fun. That's all we did. We had fun pretending to some old woman passing by that he was a selkie that had washed up on the shore."

Fergus glared at her, still red with fury.

"Yes, it was childish," Marie went on. "But what is life if we cannot embrace simple, childish joys now and then?"

"You are not a child," Fergus growled.

"No, I'm not. But I'm still capable of joy. We all are, but those rules of society that you seem so intent to embrace would have us all turn into grey automatons the moment we leave the schoolroom. Why is it so very wrong for me to live a life that makes me smile and laugh? And who deemed it inappropriate for me to converse with a man who clearly has no qualms about nudity?"

"Lady Coyle informed us that the two of you were kissing," Henrietta said, one eyebrow arched as if to call Marie out for her insolence.

Marie winced, her face so hot it felt sunburned. "Yes, well, it was an incidental kiss."

"An incidental kiss?" Shannon asked off to the side.

Marie peeked at her, suddenly wary that the women she'd been counting on to be her staunchest allies might turn against her as well.

"We were caught up in the moment," she said. "But don't you worry. Mr. Darrow was lying prone on the sand at the time, and so was I. There was no embrace and hardly any touching."

Except their lips. And Marie wasn't sure she would ever be able to forget the glorious embrace of their lips and tongues. Christian had tasted of salt and excitement. Even with his arms around her only a bit, she'd felt enveloped by him. She wasn't naïve enough to think her feelings were anything other than lust and an awakening of the flesh. But then again, she hadn't felt anything close to the stirrings Christian had given her when she'd stolen a kiss from one of the pub owners they'd sold beer to, or that handsome farmer who had offered her a nosegay in exchange for a kiss, or the footman her father had summarily dismissed after catching the two of them snogging when she was fourteen.

She shook her head to clear away the thoughts. "It

I KISSED AN EARL (AND I LIKE IT)

was just a kiss," she said. "It was fun and enjoyable, just as life should be." She nodded as if to emphasize her point.

"If it's kissing and enjoyment you want, then you're in luck," Fergus said with a scowl that sent a chill down Marie's back. "The reason we didn't have this little talk yesterday afternoon is because I was making arrangements, based on Lady Coyle's advice."

"Arrangements?" Marie's voice shook at the thought.

Fergus broke into a grin that made him look downright piratical with his eyepatch. "Congratulations, dear sister," he said. "You're engaged to be married."

"I'm—how—what?" Marie gawped at him.

"I settled the deal yesterday," Fergus said. "Before word of any of this could get out. You want to play the siren? Well, go ahead. I'm sure your new husband will be glad of it. And with any luck, you'll be with child by the end of the summer, and you'll have a wee babe to calm you down by this time next year."

"Fergus, that's—" Marie shook with rage, balling her hands into fists at her sides. "That is the cruelest, most underhanded, most vile, heartless, wicked—" Marie ran out of words strong enough to spit at her brother. Her eyes stung with anger at being bartered away like so much baggage. "I will never forgive you for—"

"Fetch your hat and meet me outside," Fergus cut her off. "We're paying a call to Kilrea Manor."

Marie's mouth hung open, but her words stopped in her throat. Kilrea Manor? Christian's home? Fergus couldn't possibly have engaged her to Christian himself that quickly, could he?

But it made sense. Christian was the one she'd committed the impropriety with. It only made sense that their families would want the two of them married off as quickly as possible after that sort of a scene. And if she were honest with herself, after seeing what she stood to gain as Christian's wife—all of it—she had to admit there were worse things that could have happened.

"This isn't fair," she said all the same, rocking back and pretending she was still angry when, in fact, her heart was racing for another reason. "This absolutely isn't fair."

"Neither is life," Fergus said, still looking like the Devil himself. "Go get your things."

Marie tilted her chin up with a sniff and stomped out of the room, but the moment she was in the hall, she broke into a run, grinning from ear to ear.

"You, sir, are a complete disgrace," Christian's father snapped, his face contorted in a grimace that proved the intensity of his words. "Have you no respect for this family or our good name?"

Christian let out an impatient breath as he watched his father pace the length of his study in front of him. "I have a great deal of respect for this family," he argued. "But I also know my place in it." A place his father had made sure he knew from the time he was a boy. An inferior place.

His father wheeled around at the end of the room and glared at him with wide eyes. "Your place in it?" He turned an incredulous look to Christian's older brother, Miles, who stood by the side of their father's huge, mahogany desk with a smug look. "Do you hear this?"

"Shameful." Miles sneered, looking as smug as always. "But then, I wouldn't expect anything more from a reprobate and exhibitionist like Christian."

"Just because I am comfortable in my own skin does not make me either an exhibitionist or a reprobate," Christian argued. Though he had a few university chums in Italy who would probably argue the point. His record for going without clothes was four days, and a lovely four days they were.

"You would never be comfortable with anything ever again if I had my way," his father bellowed, pacing back toward Christian, eyes wide. "I sent you off to Cambridge to learn more than just classics and the law, young man. I sent you there to learn your place in the hierarchy of man."

"And I learned it," Christian argued. He gripped his hands behind his back so hard that he would likely bruise his own knuckles. "I learned that there is little for the second son of a middling earl to do with himself." And he'd learned that he would never, ever be anything but an afterthought in his father's eyes. A distasteful afterthought at that. So what harm was there in him enjoying life, since he would never meet his father's exacting standards?

"You could join the army," Miles suggested with a smirk, as if he knew exactly how well that would turn out. "Or take up the cloth," he went on, unable to keep himself from laughing at the ridiculousness of the notion.

Christian sent him a flat look, hoping the idiot knew he wasn't helping. "I will gladly return to Europe," he said, glancing back to his father. "If you provide me with the financing. Because as I have also discovered, there is very little that a second son can do to earn his own income when he isn't permitted any sort of employment and his allowance is a pittance."

"Are you complaining about my generosity, boy?" his father shouted.

"No, Father, I'm not." Christian let out a breath, his shoulders sinking.

He really wasn't complaining. His father offered him more than enough to live comfortably in a small way. He wouldn't have minded living a small life either, except that he craved company. And as a member of the aristocracy, the company he was supposed to keep lived in a way that required a level of income just out of his reach.

"You know, you could always give me something to do," he said, following the line of his father's pacing with his eyes. "Something with the managing of the estate. What's this I hear about a dispute over fresh water and property boundaries between us and Ned Woodlea's estate?"

I KISSED AN EARL (AND I LIKE IT)

"The property dispute with Lord Garvagh is none of your damn business, boy," his father snapped.

Christian flinched back at the vehemence of his father's statement, raising his hands as if to appease the man. "I was merely hoping to find some sort of employment that might be of help to this family that you think I should prize and respect more than I do."

"Ah ha! So you admit that you don't respect it?" Miles said with a victorious leer.

"I said no such thing," Christian defended himself, even though it felt pointless. As the oldest son and heir to the earldom, Miles had always been an arrogant prick. He'd tortured Christian mercilessly all through their childhoods, letting Christian know exactly where he stood, both in terms of rank and with their father's affections. Indeed, even though Christian always had the sense that he was never enough for his father, he'd never truly shaken his desire to try to please the man and earn his love at last.

"Just...just tell me what I can do to make up for this sin in your eyes," he said, his heart sinking. He didn't think anything he'd done came close to being a sin. Lady Marie certainly hadn't been offended. Far from it, she'd been a delight. He'd fallen asleep with the memory of her laughter ringing in his ears the night before and the flash of her green eyes tickling every bit of his remembrance. So much so that he couldn't resist frigging himself senseless as he imagined a different way their encounter might have turned out. But those thoughts were the last thing he wanted his father to have so much as a hint of.

"You can behave yourself and do as you're told," his father said, coming to a stop in front of him with a sharp glower. "That begins with marrying."

A light of hope blossomed in Christian's chest. "You want me to marry?" he asked.

Instantly, he thought of Lady Marie. She was the daughter of an earl, after all, and his social equal. Granted, he'd only just made her acquaintance, but if he was being forced into matrimony, why not marry the woman who had sparked his imagination in such a delightful way? There had certainly been enough of an initial spark between them to suggest that they might be a brilliant match. The more he considered it, the more he was in favor of the idea.

"All right, Father," he said with a shrug, feeling as though a weight had been lifted from his shoulders. "I'll marry. In fact, I have a woman in mind who—"

"I've already arranged a marriage for you," his father cut him off.

"Arranged?" Frustration burned where hope had been inside of Christian a second before.

His father glanced at his pocket watch. "In fact, she and her brother should be here now. Come along."

His father turned sharply and gestured to Miles. The two of them started out of the room, leaving Christian stunned in their wake. He leapt into motion after them, his heart lifting again. His father had arranged for him to

I KISSED AN EARL (AND I LIKE IT)

marry, and the woman was there with her brother now? Marie had a brother. Fergus O'Shea was responsible for his sisters. It couldn't possibly be that his father had done something he might actually approve of, could it?

He marched down the hall from his father's study to the morning parlor, his heart lifting with each step. It swelled near to the point of bursting as the three of them walked into the room to find his mother already hosting what looked like a delightful tea party.

And there she was. Lady Marie looked like a dream in light green silk, her ginger hair pulled up in the latest style. Her cheeks were pink with excitement, and her eyes flashed with good humor as she sat beside his mother on the settee, entertaining her with what must have been a cheeky story, judging by his mother's amusement. There were two other people in the room, a lady and a gentleman, but Christian only had eyes for Marie. Everything was going to turn out the way it should after all.

"Ah, there you are," his mother said, rising from her seat with a smile. "I've just been listening to the most delightful story from your fiancée, Miles."

At first, Christian didn't think he'd heard right. Marie glanced in his direction, their eyes met, and it was as if the rest of the world disappeared for a moment. Even though several yards separated them, Christian felt the same rush of excitement and rightness that he'd felt the morning before, as he and Marie had played their prank on the hapless old woman. Yes, he could marry Marie. He could easily marry her. And the two of them would be happy together and—

"I'm sorry." He shook his head and dragged his eyes away from Marie to frown at his mother. "Did you say *Miles?*"

"Yes, you dolt," Miles said, shifting to stand by Christian's side with a superior smirk. "We're both getting married."

Christian's pulse kicked up as he glanced from his smug brother to his father, then on to his mother, and finally, Marie. "We are?" His voice sounded far away in his own ears.

"Yes, and what a happy day it is," his mother said. "Lord Ballymena here has agreed to have his sister, Lady Marie, marry Miles, and Lord Boleran has graciously given over the hand of his darling sister, Lady Aoife to you, Christian."

Christian's jaw dropped as his mother gestured to a pale, rather mousy-looking young woman with downcast eyes who looked as though she didn't have enough spark within her to light a match. The hopes that had towered so high within him moments before came crashing down.

CHAPTER 4

Marie gasped so hard at Lady Kilrea's revelation of who was engaged to whom that she instantly burst into a fit of coughing. She couldn't believe it. She simply couldn't believe it. But more immediately, she couldn't catch her breath.

"Good heavens, my dear, are you well?" Lady Kilrea asked, resting a maternal hand on Marie's back.

The gesture was pure and sweet, which only twisted Marie's heart in her chest and prolonged her fit. "I'm fine," she managed to croak as Lady Kilrea gestured for Lady Aoife to fetch Marie's teacup from the low table in front of the settee.

"Here you go, Lady Marie. A spot of tea will make everything well again." Lady Kilrea handed her the teacup with a worried look in her eyes. Not just a worried look, a shrewd one. The older woman glanced from Marie to Christian for a moment before focusing on helping Marie steady herself. "It must be a shock to learn you will be a countess someday."

A thousand different emotions ricocheted through Marie. Shock was indeed one of them, but it had nothing to do with her becoming a countess. She swallowed a second mouthful of tea and did her best to smile gratefully at Lady Aoife.

Lady Aoife, who looked like a porcelain doll that had been left at the back of the shelf. One that hadn't been painted vividly enough to catch anyone's interest. Lady Aoife, who could barely lift her eyes to make certain Marie wasn't choking to death, who had turned scarlet when it was announced she was betrothed to Christian. Lady Aoife, who damn well wasn't going to marry Christian Darrow if Marie had anything to say about it.

The trouble was, she *couldn't* say anything about it. Not when Fergus and Lord Kilrea were so busy congratulating themselves at the side of the gathering. Worse still, Lord Kilrea looked down at Fergus as though he were a leper and not just a man who had lost an eye and the use of his legs in a scurrilous attack. Marie wasn't sure which she hated more, the betrayal that had been hoisted on her or Lord Kilrea's condescension.

"Father, perhaps we could discuss these marital arrangements?" Christian asked into the relative silence that had followed the announcement.

"Yes, a discussion would be grand," Marie managed to croak after swallowing another mouthful of tea. She glared at Fergus as though she could bore a hole through her brother's head.

Lord Kilrea looked surprised at the hint of mutiny. "I see nothing to discuss," he said with a shrug. The way he looked at Christian was almost as harsh as the glare Fergus had for Marie. "There is a necessity of marriage. For both my sons. Suitable brides became available. What more is needed?"

"Suitable brides?" Marie said, teetering on the verge of exploding. The only thing that kept her from going off was Lady Kilrea's maternal presence at her side.

"James," she hissed at her husband. "There is no need to diminish the importance of these lovely ladies by referring to them merely as brides. As though they were chattel." She sniffed and shook her head, then smiled broadly at Marie. She turned that smile to Lady Aoife as well. "Soon they will be more than brides, they will be daughters-in-law."

A whole different kind of misery flooded Marie. It didn't take much of a stretch of the imagination to see that Lady Kilrea was lonely. Perhaps for female company in particular. The hope that shone in her eyes was devastating. And it looked rather like the mischief that had shone in Christian's eyes the day before. In fact, Marie could see that Christian favored his mother in looks and temperament, whereas his brother, Miles, took after their father.

Christian's brother Miles. To whom she was now engaged, thanks to Fergus's shenanigans.

"Fergus, dear brother," Marie said through clenched teeth, stepping away from Lady Kilrea as gently as she could. "Might I have a word with you?"

"I thought you might want to," Fergus said, the gleam of an impending fight in his one eye.

Henrietta stood by, of course, and as Marie stepped toward them, she shifted behind Fergus's chair and wheeled him to the far corner of the room.

As soon as the three of them were alone, Marie stood as close as she dared to Fergus's chair and leaned over him to hiss, "Of all the slimy, underhanded, miserable tricks."

"I told you I had arranged a marriage for you to keep you out of trouble," Fergus said, radiating anger.

"You could have engaged me to Mr. Darrow," Marie managed to push out, trembling with fury. "He was the one whose actions you found so objectionable and ruinous in the first place."

Fergus had to lean back in his chair to glare up at her. "Oh, so you think you should be *rewarded* for behaving like a hussy, do you?"

Marie bristled, eyes going wide. "You intend to punish me for life by shackling me to Lord...Lord...I don't even know the man's proper title?" she seethed.

"Lord Agivey is a perfectly decent fellow," Fergus growled in return. "And he's set to inherit the title. Most sisters would be falling all over their brothers in thanks right about now."

"I will not thank you for engaging me to a man that I

can see at once I could not possibly ever love," Marie snapped, alarmed to find herself on the edge of tears.

"Whereas you think you could love Mr. Darrow," Henrietta filled in the rest of her thought. At least Henrietta had a shred of compassion in her eyes.

Marie wanted to reply, but she feared if she opened her mouth, anything that came out of it would issue forth as a howl.

"Lord Boleran beat me to it," Fergus admitted in a low voice. "By a matter of hours, I might add."

"What?" Marie squeaked.

She glanced briefly over her shoulder to where Lord Boleran and Lady Aoife were now in conversation with Christian, his father, and his brother, Marie's wretched fiancé. Christian wore an irritated flush, but was attempting to speak politely to Lady Aoife and Lord Boleran both. He happened to look in her direction, and when their eyes met, Marie could feel the strength of his frustration in her bones. She had a feeling Christian could sense the depths of her irritation as well.

Fergus's sigh drew her attention back to her own conversation. "I came here yesterday, fully intending to marry you off to that bounder, Darrow," he said. "But as I was coming in, Boleran was just leaving. For whatever reason, he needed to marry his sister off in a hurry."

Marie blinked, glanced across to Lady Aoife, and frowned. She studied the bland wisp of a woman for a second before frowning at Fergus again. "She's not, you know, in the family way, is she?"

"I doubt it, by the looks of her," Fergus said. "And there was no chance of me asking Boleran right out."

"But really, the only reason a brother has to marry off his sister in a hurry is if she has compromised herself in some way," Henrietta said, staring pointedly at Marie.

"I did not compromise myself," Marie whispered tightly. Guilt lashed her a moment later, so she added, "Not *that* way, at least."

"It hardly matters now," Fergus said. "You made your choices and I've made mine. To save us all from disgrace and ruination, you're marrying Lord Agivey."

"I don't like the look of him," Marie grumbled. She was being sullen and petulant, she would admit as much, even though it stung her pride. But this wasn't a hand of cards or a waltz at some ball they were talking about. This was her life, her future.

She stole another look over her shoulder at Christian. He clearly wasn't any happier about the situation than she was. But once again, Marie caught sight of Lady Kilrea and the pure joy in the woman's eyes as she joined the conversation with Lady Aoife. Misery ate a hole in Marie's chest.

"I'm not sure I'll ever be able to forgive you for this, Fergus," she said in a dangerously hollow voice.

Fergus and Henrietta exchanged a wary look.

"Perhaps this whole plot was entered into with a bit too much haste," Henrietta said. "Marie likes Mr. Darrow, not his brother."

"There's nothing I can do about it," Fergus argued. "The agreement has already been made."

"How many times have I told you not to enter into business dealings while angry, darling?" Henrietta scolded Fergus.

"Undo it," Marie said, balling her hands into fists at her sides. "I don't care what it costs you, undo the betrothal this instant."

"And if that is even possible?" Fergus stared up at her, his one eye sharp. "I suppose you want me to convince Lord Boleran to undo his sister's engagement to your Mr. Darrow as well?"

Marie winced. "Lord Boleran is a marquess. You're just an earl. Surely, Lord Kilrea would want his eldest son and heir to marry the sister of a marquess instead of an earl's wicked sister."

"Kilrea was a little too intrigued by my English connections," Fergus said with a frown. "Not to mention Henrietta's connections. Boleran might be a marquess, but he doesn't have the connections I do."

"Dammit." Marie stomped her foot, feeling far too boxed in by the machinations of an aristocracy she had never had the time of day for.

Her tiny outburst caught the attention of everyone at the other end of the room. Lady Kilrea's face pinched with regret, which spilled even more guilt through Marie. Lady Aoife kept her head down, of course, but Lord Boleran and Lord Agivey frowned in disapproval. The sight of her fiancé's frown sent dread pooling in Marie's stomach. That was what she had to look forward to?

Christian's expression was the only one that hardened into a sense of purpose. But when he attempted to step away from his group and head across the room to Marie's, his father caught his arm and jerked him to a stop. Christian remained off-balance for the amount of time it took for his father to whisper something to him. After that, Christian's expression flattened and he stood straighter, turning back to the conversation in front of him.

Not that there was much conversation after the awkward interruption.

"Well, isn't this a fine kettle of fish," Marie said, shaking her head in annoyance and stepping away from her brother and sister-in-law. She couldn't think of anything to do in the moment to get out of the horrific situation. The only thing she could do was to gather more information so she could figure out a way to save her skin.

That meant putting on a polite smile and returning to Lady Kilrea's side. Her potential future mother-in-law was the only bright spot in the muddle, so she would focus her efforts there to start.

"You must be so pleased to have daughters-in-law on the horizon, my lady," Marie opened the conversation with the woman. She reluctantly included Lady Aoife in the small circle they made adjacent to the conversation the men carried on with. Henrietta wheeled Fergus into that conversation, then joined the women herself.

"I am," Lady Kilrea said, placing a hand on her chest and glancing fondly from Marie to Lady Aoife. "I have had so little female companionship in my day, you see."

"Oh? Do you not have sisters?" Henrietta asked.

"Alas, I had a younger sister, Evelyn," Lady Kilrea sighed. "She was a year younger than me, but the poor thing died of a fever when she was ten." The tragedy had clearly happened decades ago, but Lady Kilrea teared up all the same. "And I have given birth to two beautiful baby girls in my time," she went on. "Sadly, neither of them made it out of the cradle." She glanced between Marie and Lady Aoife again. "They would be about your ages now, I believe."

Marie wanted to burst into tears herself at the revelation. She wanted to throw back her head and wail. Lady Kilrea was far too precious and much too fragile for her to callously throw over her son. She couldn't possibly deny the woman the love that she must have felt she'd been missing her whole life. Even though it meant she was about to enter a prison that she would never be able to escape.

A prison that would be made a thousand times worse by the proximity it would bring her to Christian. She glanced to the side, finding Christian staring at her with his lips pressed shut and anger in his eyes. Marie felt that anger in her soul. It was bloody well unfair of the fates and their male relatives to ruin their lives before they'd even had a chance to begin. And yes, she was fully aware of the reality that she had only just met Christian. It was impossible for her to have developed feelings for him worth building a lifetime on after one encounter, no matter how jolly and…and naked that encounter had been. But that didn't stop her from wanting to scream over the whole thing.

"It's only right that Miles marry first," Lady Kilrea said, pulling Marie's attention back to the matter at hand. "He is the eldest, after all. And I believe my husband is in something of a hurry to have the wedding. You wouldn't mind if it was held in September, would you, my dear?"

Marie smiled, in spite of the fact that she wanted to weep. "Not at all, my lady."

Lady Kilrea beamed, then turned to Lady Aoife. "And yours shall be a Christmas wedding. Won't that be grand."

"Lovely, my lady," Lady Aoife muttered, eyes downcast and cheeks pink.

"What's this I hear about a September and a Christmas wedding?" Lord Kilrea asked. He managed to subtly maneuver them all so that they formed one large conversation.

"Are we certain September is soon enough?" Lord Agivey asked, leering at Marie.

Christian looked as though he wanted to throttle his brother.

"We'll have a party to announce the engagements immediately," Lord Kilrea said. "An engagement party is as good as a wedding in some circles." He laughed proudly, as though he'd accomplished a coup.

"Will the engagement party happen here?" Fergus asked. "Or would you rather have it at Dunegard Castle?"

"Oh, at the castle, of course." Lord Kilrea's eyes shone, as though the mere thought of being seen hosting a party at a castle would raise his standing in Ireland and England both.

Fergus sent Henrietta a look as though the two of them knew precisely what the man was thinking. Marie would have joined in, but the reality of having a party planned for her engagement to a man who had yet to actually speak to her directly had chased any hope of seeing humor in the situation right out of her. She peeked desperately at Christian. He felt like her only ally in the dire situation.

"Excuse me, Father," Christian said, glancing away from Marie. "Could I have a word with Lord Boleran?"

"Yes, of course," Lord Kilrea said with a slight frown.

Marie frowned as well. As Christian stepped away with Lord Boleran, she felt as though she'd lost her last ally. Only when Christian sent a short look back over his shoulder to her, a hint of mischief in his eyes, did Marie consider that he was up to something. Perhaps his efforts to break away from the group at large had nothing to do with speaking to his fiancée's brother—dear God, that was what Lord Boleran was to him now—and more to do with getting away from his father. If that were the case, she needed to find a way out as well.

"Excuse me, my lady," she said, leaning close to Lady Kilrea's ear. "Could I make use of your retiring room?"

Lady Kilrea blinked at her for a moment, then seemed to understand. "Yes, yes, of course." She waved to one of the maids—who were standing at the ready around the perimeter of the room. "Laura, please show Lady Marie to the facilities," she asked one of the maids in a hush.

It was all a lot of fuss to get Marie out of the room, but she didn't care. As soon as the maid led her down the hall to the water closet, Marie thanked the girl, then pretended to go about her business, shutting herself in the tiny room. A scant few seconds later, she popped her head back out into the hall. If she'd guessed correctly, Christian would slip out of the parlor as well.

She was right. Her heart sang with joy and mischief as Christian stepped into the hall. He saw her head peeking out from the door and broke into a wide grin, picking up his pace. Within seconds, he'd slipped into the water closet with her.

"I'd say we're in a bit of a tight situation," Marie whispered as the two of them squeezed into the small space. The water closet was bigger than a bedroom closet, but not by much. On top of that, it was jammed with modern plumbing. The space had obviously been carved into the existing structure of a house that had been designed before the invention of indoor plumbing, but it had been designed poorly.

Not that Marie was in the mood to complain about

the necessity of wedging herself closer to Christian at the moment.

"This is more than a tight situation," Christian said, his expression seeming to have a hard time deciding whether to be jolly or morose. "This is an emergency."

"I could strangle my brother for pushing me off on your brother this way," Marie said, moving her arms restlessly, not sure where to put them.

Christian settled the matter for her by grasping her hands and holding them between their bodies. "And I had no idea who Lady Aoife was, let alone that my father thought she'd be a suitable match."

"Did you learn anything from her brother just now?" Marie asked, hope rising in her. "Why he's in such a rush to marry off his sister?"

"No," Christian said with a sigh. "Only that he's adamant his sister marry as soon as possible. Which is highly suspicious, if you ask me."

"Definitely suspicious," Marie echoed. "Why anyone would need to marry in such a rush is beyond me."

Christian's eyes suddenly danced with mischief and delight. Marie found herself uncommonly aware of the closeness of the water closet and how necessary it was for them to stand almost flush against each other.

"I'm not opposed to the idea of marriage in general, you know," Christian said, the warmth in his eyes growing. "It has its uses."

"It certainly does," Marie agreed. The water closet was amazingly warm all of a sudden, and she had the uncanny urge to giggle in spite of the muddle they were in. "I wouldn't mind marrying myself," she went on. "Provided I was allowed to choose my groom."

"My feelings precisely." Christian nodded. "That is to say, marriage isn't something I had even thought to contemplate at this stage of my life, but if I were in the market for a wife—"

"And if I felt as though now were the right time in my life—" Marie added.

"Who is to say what exciting and vivacious bride I might choose?"

"I might be persuaded to shackle myself to someone who keeps me on my toes," Marie agreed.

"If it was an absolute necessity," Christian said.

"If it were a requirement that the decision be made immediately," Marie said.

"I might find it within my power to—"

She lifted to her toes and threw her arms over his shoulders, kissing him with all the daring and desperation she felt. He let out a wild sound of acceptance and relief, kissing her back and wrapping his arms around her the way Marie had wanted him to the day before. It was sheer madness for them to kiss that way, in a water closet located right in the center of his house when both of their families were only rooms away, but Marie didn't care. His body was scintillating against hers, and the emotions and urges his hungry mouth inspired in her were headier than the finest beer.

I KISSED AN EARL (AND I LIKE IT)

"Wait," Christian gasped, breaking their kiss. "This is thoroughly mad, isn't it."

"That we're kissing in a water closet mere minutes after being engaged against our will to other people?" Marie suggested.

"Yes?" His grin widened. "That and considering we only met yesterday."

"It is." Marie nodded, staring at his kiss-reddened lips. "It's completely mad." She launched into him again, throwing her whole heart into kissing him and exploring him with her tongue.

"Good," he said between desperate kisses. "I always wanted to do something hair-brained and shocking."

"I'm sure you've done plenty of hair-brained things and will do many more that are twice as shocking," she cooed as she threaded her fingers through his hair. All her life, she'd been warned about the allure and seduction of the flesh. She'd been told that sensuality was powerful and could lead a woman down a dangerous path in no time. As she kissed Christian, loving every moment of his mouth against hers and his hands exploring her sides, she knew it was true.

"You're not marrying my brother," Christian said at last, breathless and alive with energy.

"And you're not marrying Lady Aoife," Marie told him. "But how do we stop the weddings?"

"We can start by stopping the engagement party." Christian had the same mischievous light in his eyes that he'd had when he asked her to play the prank on the old woman the day before.

"Yes," Marie said. "Whatever wickedness you're plotting, I say yes."

"Good." He kissed her once more, soundly, then leaned back. "I have an idea. I'm sure by the time we get back to the parlor, my father will have set a date for the engagement party. Whatever day that is, I want you to meet me in the carriage house here, at Kilrea Manor."

"The carriage house?" Marie blinked up at him.

Christian's grin widened. "They can't announce our engagement if they never make it to the party."

Marie sucked in a breath, then let it out in a giggle. "Whatever you're plotting, it's brilliant." She kissed him again, more certain than ever that it was possible to know in an instant when you'd met your match.

CHAPTER 5

Of all the things that Christian learned at university, the most useful was to hope for the best but to plan for the worst. He had a plan to free both himself and Marie from their painfully unsuitable betrothals—a jolly, high-spirited plan at that—but he wasn't the sort to prank his way out of his problems without trying every rational and reasonable means to fix things first.

Luckily for him—and for Marie—the fortnight that followed the revelation of their horrific engagements involved the three families seeing each other on an almost daily basis. That meant he and Marie were able to spend a surprising amount of time together, though none of it spent alone. In a way, Christian didn't mind. Being thrown into crowded social situations with Marie meant that he was able to talk to her, to get to know her better. And he liked everything he learned about her—about how intelligent she actually was and how industrious, about her shockingly modern views of the world, and her good heart. The way she took to his mother, and his mother to her, was even more encouragement for Christian.

By the morning of the engagement party at Dunegard Castle, he was convinced that his initial impressions of Marie as being the perfect woman for him in every way were correct. Which meant he wasn't going to stand by and watch both Marie and himself be treated like pawns in a chess game.

"Surely, Father, you must see that Miles and Lady Marie have nothing at all in common," he argued while pacing his father's office hours before the family was due to leave Kilrea Manor for the party. "Miles has barely spoken two words to her since you announced the engagement."

"I have nothing to say to her," Miles argued without glancing up at Christian. He leaned against his father's desk, inspecting his nails—which had the perfection of a man who hadn't done a lick of manual labor in his life.

"You don't need to say anything to her," their father added without looking up from the papers on his desk.

"That is preposterous." Christian glared at his brother. "One should have a loving, or at least cordial, relationship with one's wife."

"And is that why you've been paying Lady Aoife so much mind?" Miles asked with a sharp smirk.

Christian let out a breath, trying not to let the guilt of

largely ignoring the woman he was supposed to marry bother him. He had no intention of ever going through with that marriage, after all. "Lady Aoife is difficult to converse with," he said in a low voice. "She doesn't seem to have any opinions. She's always glancing out the window as though she'd rather be somewhere else."

"At least my fiancée is interested in conversation," Miles snorted, as though he'd scored a point against Christian.

Christian clenched his jaw and glared at his brother. They'd battled for everything from pudding to attention for as long as he could remember. And for what? There were no rules saying a man had to be close to his brother. The urge to best Miles was still there, though, but before he could tell him off, their father said, "Conversation in a marriage is irrelevant. All you need is a hostess to entertain your company and a womb to bear your heir."

Christian gaped at his father, disgust welling up in him. "What kind of an antiquated, misogynistic opinion is that?"

The vehemence of his question was enough to startle his father out of the business of the estate spread across his desk. "I beg your pardon?" he seethed.

"Is your head so buried in disputed estate boundaries and cheating our neighbors that you haven't stopped to realize how important women are in our world?" Christian demanded.

Miles snorted. "They're important in the bedroom,

all right. Although I'd just as soon have a mistress. A wife could never satisfy my particular tastes."

Christian shook his head, unable to believe what he was hearing. "Women are being admitted to universities now," he said. "They are entering the workforce in larger numbers than ever before. They own businesses, manage estates. Some even hold public office."

"No woman with any sort of breeding does anything half so scandalous," his father huffed, looking genuinely put out. "And no son of mine will speak of such atrocities, let alone champion them."

"I cannot believe what I am hearing," Christian said. "I knew your opinions were old-fashioned, Father, but I had no idea they were so backwards."

"Backwards?" His father snorted with laughter. "This from a rapscallion who waltzes about the countryside in his altogether, leading daughters of the aristocracy astray."

"I was having fun." Christian raised his voice. When both his father and Miles sneered, he went on with, "Life is meant to be fun. It is meant to be filled with joy and laughter."

"It is meant to be filled with diligence, hard work, and the maintenance of proper order," his father argued.

A strange sort of pain filled Christian. His father and brother would never understand him. He shouldn't need their understanding or approval, but, damn him, he did. Even if he didn't have the slightest idea how to gain that approval.

"Life is meant to be happy. Even you deserve to be happy." He flung out a hand toward Miles. "These marriages you propose will bring about misery. I won't stand by and let them happen."

"You have no choice." His father rose abruptly, leaning forward over his desk and glaring at Christian. "I am your father," he said, snapping each word. "I rule this family. God has ordained it to be so. You will do as you are told or you will be flung out like so much chaff."

"You are making a mistake," Christian countered. "A mistake that will have all of us cursing your name for decades to come."

"Then curse me." His father shrugged as though he didn't care. "Just do as I say."

Never before had Christian had such a strong urge to strike his own father. The man was blinded by his pride. Worse still, Christian knew the louder he protested the betrothals, the more his father would dig in his heels. It seemed as though reason and logic couldn't win out against arrogance and cynicism after all.

Too aggravated to say anything more, Christian turned and stormed out of the room. Miles sniggered at him as he went, which only darkened Christian's heart more. If he couldn't talk his and Marie's way out of the betrothals, he would have to resort to pranks after all.

By the time he reached the carriage house, his frustration had coalesced into wicked purpose. It was a longshot, but if he aggravated his father to the point of madness by making his every living moment a lesson in obstruction, maybe he could convince the man to see things his way.

"You look like sunshine and roses." Marie startled him by pushing away from the carriage house's door and stepping toward him.

A rush of joy cut through the darkness growing inside of Christian and he breathed a sigh of relief. "You remembered," he said, moving toward her and pulling her into his arms.

"How could I forget?" she asked with a saucy smile, sliding her arms over his shoulders and playing with strands of his hair.

Marie made him happy. That was all that mattered. They were completely mad to carry on the way they had, they were risking so much more than just their reputations by encouraging the spark between them, but Christian wouldn't have had it any other way. It settled him so deeply that he risked kissing her right then and there, in the doorway of the carriage house, where anyone might have seen them.

"Delightful," Marie sighed as their kiss ended. A moment later, her eyes widened and her smile grew. "So why did you want me to meet you here, of all places? Are we going to run away together and live the life of vagabonds, traveling the world and constantly running from our families?"

Christian laughed aloud, heart full. "No, but I like that as a secondary idea." He stepped away from her, taking her hand and leading her deeper into the line of parked carriages housed in the old building. "Is everything still set up for the party at your brother's house later?" he asked, heading for the carriage his father favored for paying calls. It was a large, black-lacquered thing with the family crest painted on the doors. Granted, all of his father's carriages were large, black-lacquered things with the crest on the doors, but this one was the largest.

Marie huffed and leaned against the carriage when Christian let go of her hand. "Yes, unfortunately. I've begged and pleaded with Fergus to renege on the engagement. I've wept and I've cajoled. I even told him exactly why I would rather die than marry your brother."

Christian glanced over his shoulder at her as he fetched the box of tools for maintaining the carriages from one of the shelves at the side of the room. "And why would you rather die than marry my brother?" he asked with a teasing grin.

Marie's answering look—wicked as the day was long—made Christian's heart swell. It made other things swell as well. That gave him ideas far beyond the initial prank he had in store.

"I think you know what my reasons are," she said, flickering one eyebrow at him as he returned to the carriage.

He laughed, then dropped to squat and stare at the underside of the carriage. "If you continue to look at me like that, Lady Marie, you'll put notions into my head that would make even the sauciest of souls blush."

"I certainly hope so," she hummed. A pause followed, then she asked in a far more serious voice, "What are you doing?"

"Putting my plan in motion," Christian said, taking a wrench from the toolbox and going to work on the bolts that held the carriage's axel together.

Marie squatted by his side, her eyes round as she watched him work. "Good Lord. If you do that, the wheels will fall off."

"That is the general idea." Christian sent her a naughty wink.

Marie clapped a hand over her mouth to hide her giggle. "I knew you were impish," she said a moment later, "but I had no idea you were downright bad."

"I'm clever," he said, loosening another bolt, then leaning closer to Marie, flickering one eyebrow. "But I can be bad, if that's what you want me to be."

Marie's answering laugh shot straight to his groin as he went back to work, loosening bolts. "But how do you know this is the carriage your father will take to the party?" she asked, following him around the carriage as he worked.

"This is his favorite," Christian reasoned. "And I'm not disabling it outright. If I've calculated correctly, the carriage will hold together long enough to get them away from the house before the wheels fall off. That way, they'll be forced to walk back here to fetch another carriage. With any luck, they'll give up entirely and call the whole party off."

"What a delightfully mad-capped plan," Marie asked. "I hope it works."

"It will," he promised her with a deep earnestness. "You won't have to marry Miles, I swear."

It was mad, but Christian disabling his father's carriage might have been the sweetest thing anyone had ever done for Marie. She asked Christian questions about his experience with carriages as he finished loosening bolts underneath the thing, then stood to replace the tools and wipe his hands.

"I never was one to stand idly by and let other people solve my problems," he explained once he was done, as the two of them headed outside to where Marie had left her bicycle. "When I was traveling with my friends in Europe after university, I found it necessary to repair the carriage we'd hired on a regular basis. As it turns out, that was a useful skill to have."

"So, if your father tosses you out on your ear for defying him, you'll be able to find work as a mechanic," Marie said with a wry grin.

"I will never want for anything," Christian replied with mock seriousness.

Marie laughed, and her heart felt light. In the last fortnight, Fergus had insisted she spend as much time with the Darrow family as possible, ostensibly to get to know her fiancé better. Fergus foolishly believed that if Marie liked one brother, she would like the other as well.

But Miles was nothing like Christian, and Christian was the most magnificent man she'd ever met. The days they'd spent together, even though they hadn't been alone, had confirmed every initial feeling she'd had for the man. She'd be damned if she married anyone but Christian Darrow.

"What do we do now?" she asked grabbing the handlebars of her bicycle and walking it around so that it pointed toward the drive leading away from the carriage house and stables. "The party isn't for several hours."

Christian swayed closer to her, even though the bicycle stood between them. "We'll just have to find something to occupy ourselves," he said with a look of such mischief that Marie's insides threatened to turn to jelly. Christian wasn't just handsome and clever, he made her want to throw every bit of caution and propriety to the wind so that she could explore all the things that were supposed to be forbidden with him.

"We could go for a bicycle ride," she suggested. "If you owned a bicycle."

"I don't," he said, deflating. A moment later, he brightened all over again. "But we could try something I saw some of the girls in Southern France do with their beaux."

Something about the sentence sent a giddy thrill through Marie's gut. "I think I would rather enjoy attempting things that girls in Southern France do with their beaux."

Christian's eyes heated, as though he knew exactly what she meant. "Come on, then."

He reached for her hand—or rather, he took the handlebars of the bicycle from her. Before Marie could figure out what he was doing, he'd mounted the bicycle and was ready to ride.

"You can ride on the handlebars," he said with a wink.

Marie's jaw dropped, and a spike of genuine worry twisted around her gut. "Really? Is that even possible?"

"Like I said, girls in France do it all the time," Christian said.

"And I won't be outdone by girls in France," Marie said, mostly to herself.

It took a few tries for her to figure out how to climb up onto the handlebars. Christian helped her, but then they had to spend a few minutes figuring out how to tuck her skirts in so that they wouldn't catch in the wheels. After a few false starts, they coordinated their actions enough for Christian to peddle the bicycle forward with Marie as a passenger.

Once they got the hang of things, Christian picked up speed as they sailed away from Kilrea Manor and onto the road. Marie was dreadfully uncomfortable with the solid handlebar wedged against her unmentionable bits. The wind threatened to rip her hat clean off her head, so she had to hold it with one hand and grip any part of the bicycle she could reach for dear life with her other hand.

But they managed to keep their balance as they shot off into the green countryside.

"Where are we going?" Christian shouted over the wind as they rolled along at a speed that had Marie's heart in her throat.

She thought fast, glancing around as best she could. All she wanted to do was spend time with Christian. Alone. That would never happen if they went on to Dunegard Castle, or even into one of the towns and villages nearby. There was really only one option.

"To the cottage," she said over her shoulder as best she could without losing her balance.

"The cottage?" Christian asked.

"You'll see."

She directed him along the road, telling him when to turn and which way to go. The ride was made extra thrilling, knowing they were headed somewhere they truly shouldn't have been, and that they would be there alone. All the same, Marie was grateful to see her home for the last few years peek out from around the corner as they neared the cliff where it was perched. She and her sisters had left the place less than a month before, and even though Fergus had forbidden it, they had all been checking in on their home to make sure it was in good order.

"This place is lovely," Christian said, glancing around after Marie hopped off the bicycle—or rather, stumbled clumsily and nearly ended up splayed in the grass. "And you say you used to live here?"

"Up until very recently," Marie confirmed, pointing to where Christian could prop the bicycle against the side of the house. No other bicycles were there, indicating that her sisters weren't there either. They were probably all at the castle, preparing for the party. "Fergus made us move back to the house so that he could marry us all off mercilessly."

"Mercilessly," Christian repeated teasingly as Marie unlocked the cottage's front door and led him inside. "It's a good thing we aren't going to let that happen," he said.

"Isn't it, though?" Marie laughed.

Christian took in the front rooms of the house instead of replying. Everything was the way Marie and her sisters had left it while living there. The kitchen was still set up for brewing beer, which came as no surprise to Marie. She had a sneaking suspicion Shannon had kept their scandalous enterprise going since they'd all moved back to the castle. It was a pleasure to show Christian around the beloved place. Judging by the spark in his eyes, he was impressed by what he saw.

"What a cozy little home," he said with genuine feeling.

"I love it," Marie said with a sigh.

"As do I." Christian glanced to her, his smile growing. "The walls are filled with happiness."

Marie beamed at the compliment. "They are," she agreed. "We were always happy here."

"And did you bring gentlemen to your cozy little

home?" he asked, slinking closer to her as they reached the main downstairs parlor.

Marie bit her lip, letting herself slide into his offered embrace. "Not once." She tilted her head to the side. "Though heaven knows why I didn't think of that sooner."

He laughed deep in his throat, and Marie thought she might explode right out of her skin. He followed that with a searing kiss, his mouth slanting over hers and devouring her with tender passion. He was easily the finest kisser Marie had ever known. He made her wish she'd never kissed another man before. Then again, after the way he teased her with his lips and tongue, his hands brushing her sides and caressing her breasts, she didn't think she would ever be able to remember another man as long as she lived.

"Do you know," he began in a low purr, "I've just had a thought about a practically fool-proof way my father and your brother could be convinced to call off our erstwhile betrothals and let us marry each other."

Marie sucked in a breath. It was the first time either of them had spoken outright about the possibility of marrying each other. She'd known in her heart it was what she truly wanted, but hearing the words spoken aloud thrilled her beyond measure.

"What way is that?" she asked breathlessly.

He inched back enough to gaze into her eyes with fire. "If I were to thoroughly ruin you, I don't see how they could say no to our union."

I KISSED AN EARL (AND I LIKE IT)

Marie stared back at him, her blood racing through her veins. "Heavens, Mr. Darrow. Are you actually suggesting whisking me upstairs to my old bedroom and ravishing me?"

"Yes, that's exactly what I'm suggesting," he said with a mischievous sparkle in his eyes.

"That would certainly convince everyone to back away from the ill-advised betrothals they've thrown us into," she said, sinking against him. She loved the feeling of his body against hers, and if she wasn't mistaken, part of his body was already excited by the idea of sneaking upstairs with her.

"Like I said." He kissed her lightly. "A fool-proof plan." He kissed her again.

"How could I possibly say no to a fool-proof plan?" Marie asked, grinning from ear to ear. She didn't wait for him to continue with the banter or ask for some sort of permission. She broke away from him, grabbing his hand, and dashed down the hall to the stairs with him.

Christian's laughter as they hurried up the stairs went straight to Marie's head. There was something innocent and almost childlike about the way they took the stairs two at a time, hardly pausing for breath when they reached Marie's room at the top. As soon as they crossed Marie's threshold, Christian shut the door behind them with his foot, then yanked Marie into his arms for another kiss. It was absolute joy, unfettered desire, and everything Marie could have hoped for. Whether society approved or not, she had what she wanted in her arms, and, like a child with a toy, she was determined to get the most enjoyment out of the situation that she could.

"I don't suppose I should ask whether you're sure about this," Christian said as Marie peeled his jacket from his shoulders and fumbled with the buttons of his waistcoat.

"Of course not," she gasped, wriggling so that he had better access to the buttons lining the front of her blouse. "When I know what I want, I know what I want. And I want you."

"Thank God," he groaned, taking a moment to wriggle out of his waistcoat, then tug his shirt out of his trousers and off over his head. "Because all I want is you too."

Marie made a sensual sound of approval in her throat, then spread her hands across his broad chest, loving the feel of his hair against her fingers. He was so perfectly masculine in every way. She felt as though she'd waited a lifetime to explore a man's body, and nothing felt more perfect than that body belonging to Christian. She couldn't get enough of touching him, and leaned in to bring her lips to his shoulder and collarbone. He let out a sound of approval, pausing in his clumsy efforts to undress her, and let her kiss and nip at his skin.

"I'm not sure if this is going to be the longest and most amazing experience of my life or if it'll be over before we've truly begun," he laughed. That laughter caught in his throat and turned into a groan as she reached into his trousers.

She gasped as well, biting her lip as she stroked her hand along his powerful length. She'd seen his penis in the light of day, glittering with sea water and sunshine, and she'd had the barest hint of what it might look like when he was genuinely aroused. Feeling that arousal as it grew and filled him out left her with an aching, restless sensation deep in her core.

"I'm not sure if I care how long it lasts, as long as it happens," she panted, leaning back to meet his eyes.

Christian laughed, joy and lust radiating from him. "Oh, you'll mind."

"Will I?" she asked with a coquettish arch of one eyebrow.

"Believe me," he said, finishing with the buttons of her blouse and pushing it open. "Once we get going, you'll want it to last forever."

"I like the sound of that." She fumbled with the fastenings of his trousers.

He paused after pulling her blouse from her skirt. "Perhaps not the first time." He winced. "Have you ever been with a man before?"

"No," she answered honestly, her heart thudding against her ribs as the gravity of what they were doing hit her.

"Then maybe rushing through things this first time would be best," he said.

She blinked, hands hovering over the hot hardness beneath his trousers. "Why?"

"The first time might not be that…comfortable," he warned her.

"Oh, I've heard all about that," Marie laughed. "But if you want to charge through and just get it over with—"

"The last thing I want to do is just get it over with," he laughed, continuing to undress her.

"Then by all means, take your time." Marie caught her breath as he reached around to tug at the drawstring holding her skirts in place.

The one thing they didn't take their time doing was undressing. It was far easier for him to shed his clothes—something she had a feeling he did on a regular basis, judging by how fast they dropped off him. She only had a moment to bite her lip and appreciate the pure, male glory of his erection as framed against his lean hips and flat abdomen. Her clothes took far more effort to remove and required her turning her back to him far more than she wanted to.

But at last, they were both as naked as the day they were born. They spilled into Marie's bed, panting and reaching for each other.

"You're beautiful," Christian sighed, stroking his hands across her sides and treating her breasts to feather-light touches. "I'm not sure I'll ever be able to get enough of you."

"If our plot works, you will have all the time in the world to get as much as you'd like," she told him, running her fingers through his hair.

"It still wouldn't be enough." He bent down to

I KISSED AN EARL (AND I LIKE IT)

capture her mouth, kissing her until her head spun and her body throbbed.

He didn't stop there. As glorious as his kisses were and as much as they enflamed her, it was his hands that made her writhe against him, aching for everything. He caressed her breasts, thumbing her nipples and then pinching them just enough to have her arching off the bed and gasping at the pleasure.

"I don't know how we waited so long for this," Christian panted as his hands traveled down across the flat of her stomach to delve between her legs.

"So long? We've only known each other for—oh!"

She nearly arched off the bed as his fingers stroked the wetness of her sex. She'd pleasured herself plenty of times before, but it was nothing to the expert skill of his fingers teasing and arousing her. He didn't hesitate in the slightest, thrusting first one and then two fingers inside of her to test her readiness. She was more than ready from the start, but he worked her into a need that was so desperate she thought she might come out of her skin.

That was only the beginning. With his fingers still thrusting inside of her, he positioned his thumb to rake across her clitoris. Within seconds, Marie came apart in a burst of light and pleasure. She sighed loudly at the sensations that throbbed through her, then realized Christian was groaning with triumph as well. He'd done that to her, and she had never been more overawed in her life.

As if he had a sixth sense for timing, he shifted his

body over hers, nudging her thighs open, then thrusting inside of her while she was still transported by the pleasure of her orgasm. He was so quick and decisive that the moment of shock her body experienced at his invasion felt like nothing more than a bump in the road, easily forgotten as the journey continued.

"Oh, Christian," she gasped as he moved inside her. "That's...that's...." She lost the ability to form words entirely and let out a long sigh as she moved with him.

"Marie," he gasped against her ear as his motions sped up.

It was a revelation. Marie gripped his back with her fingertips, wrapping her legs around his hips as he thrust harder and harder, until his whole body tensed and he let out a shattering sound of pleasure. Warmth and affection filled her as he spilled himself deep inside of her. It was the most amazing sensation she'd ever felt, and in echo of what he'd said earlier, she didn't ever want it to end.

But the hazy contentment that settled over them once it was done was almost as good as the act itself. She'd never felt closer to anyone in her life. Christian pulled out of her and settled at her side, then kissed her with a new, protective kind of affection that made her feel as though the sun had come out after a stormy day. She wrapped her arms around him and kissed him back, paying no mind to how sweaty and overheated they both were. There was nothing in the world better than feeling so connected to the man she knew she would move heaven and earth to spend the rest of her life with.

I KISSED AN EARL (AND I LIKE IT)

"Are you all right?" Christian managed to squeeze out a few minutes later. "I didn't hurt you much, did I?"

"You didn't hurt me at all," Marie laughed. "You can do that again whenever you'd like."

Christian laughed, snuggling against her side as though he would settle in for a nap. "With any luck, once we explain to our families what we've done, they'll let us continue on like this forever."

Marie hummed in approval at the thought, but she couldn't keep her eyes open. Neither could Christian, apparently. They drifted off into a contented sleep.

Of course, that contentment vanished in a snap when they awoke more than an hour later.

"Thank God I wound the clocks when I stopped by yesterday," Marie said, leaping out of bed and going to check the clock on her mantel to confirm the time. "We're going to be so, so late for our own party."

"If the party happens at all," Christian laughed, climbing out of bed behind her. Marie took a moment to drink in the sight of him. She could appreciate his naked form even more now, knowing what he was capable of. "Hopefully my little sabotage worked."

"Hopefully," Marie repeated.

Half an hour later, they discovered that Christian's prank had worked, but not as he'd intended. They'd washed and dressed in a hurry, fetched Marie's bicycle, and sped back along the road to Dunegard Castle. The ride was even more uncomfortable for Marie on the way back than it had been before, but just as she was close to complaining about it, she spotted something in the distance that stopped her words and her breath in her throat.

"Oh, no!" She gestured for Christian to stop the bicycle, and they both dismounted. "No!"

Ahead of them on the road and scattered for several yards to either side were broken and twisted pieces of black-lacquered, splintered wood and twisted metal. Two horses writhed and screamed in the grass as the inhabitants of a second carriage got out to check the wreckage of the first. Along with the carnage of the wrecked carriage, Marie spotted four broken and splayed bodies.

CHAPTER 6

The edges of Christian's vision blurred and his stomach lurched as his mind attempted to adjust to what he was seeing spread out across the road in front of him and Marie. He hardly felt Marie's hand grip his arm or the bicycle beneath him as he stared at the wreck of his father's carriage. For a moment, he was frozen, unable to hear Marie's cry of alarm or the shouts from the people from the second carriage that had stopped behind the wreck. A farmer's wagon was also speeding toward the scene, and the driver of the second carriage ran to meet it. But all Christian could see were the bodies spread through the wreckage.

They were completely still.

He knew in an instant what had happened, knew it and felt he might be crushed by it. An odd, strangled cry sounded somewhere in the distance. Only after he felt it burn in his lungs did he realize that the sound came from him.

"Christian." Marie's voice cut through the thundering heaviness around him.

He turned his head slowly to look at her. Her beautiful face was pinched in horror. That was enough to snap him out of his shock.

He sucked in a breath, scrambling away from the bicycle and Marie. As fast as he could, he dashed toward the wreckage.

"Stand back," the man who had reached the scene first warned him, holding up a hand.

Christian's fogged brain was slow to recognize him as Lord Boleran, which was ridiculous. He'd spent the better part of the past fortnight socializing with the man. It was a bad sign that his mind was too fractured to see Boleran as an individual and not just another part of the nightmare unfolding in front of him.

"I mean it, my lord, stand back," Boleran repeated.

"No." Christian stumbled forward in spite of Boleran's efforts to keep him away from what he knew he'd see.

The carriage was utterly destroyed, as though someone had fired a cannon shot into it. Even the metal of the axel had twisted and snapped in places. But that wasn't what snagged his attention and wouldn't let him look away. His father's body lay curled sickly around a spoke from one of the wheels. His eyes were frozen open in shock, and already his skin was pale. Blood dripped from the corner of his mouth. Several yards to the side, his brother lay on his back, his neck bent at an impossible angle. There was no blood around Miles, but it was glaringly obvious that he was as dead as their father. The driver's body was splayed far enough from the wreckage to suggest he'd been thrown with some force.

Dead. All three of them dead. Because of a carriage wreck. A wreck Christian had caused.

"My lord, come away." Boleran was behind him an instant later, resting a hand on his shoulder.

"My mother," Christian said, the words coming out in a croak.

"My lord, she's—"

Christian shrugged Boleran off, dashing to the patch of grass several yards away where his mother lay in a crumpled heap, her formal gown like a pillow around her. "Mother," he shouted, falling to his knees and reaching for her.

His efforts were met by the faintest of groans and a subtle shift from his mother. It was enough for Christian to cry out hysterically, "She's alive! Somebody fetch a doctor. Fetch a doctor at once!"

He tried to gather her in his arms, but Boleran was on him again, holding his arms back. "Don't move her, my lord," he said. "She may have internal injuries. Moving her may kill her. Wait for the doctor."

"He's been sent for," someone shouted behind Christian.

"I want my mother," Christian wailed, struggling

against Boleran and scrambling for his mother's frail and broken form. "Please, please."

"Let him hold her," Marie's shaky voice said from somewhere behind him. The joy he felt at hearing her voice quickly faded to guilt and misery. He was responsible for killing his father and brother—and perhaps his mother too—and he'd done it with Marie in mind.

"My lord, you really should wait for the doctor," Boleran went on as Christian ignored him to hunch over his mother, cradling her as best he could while touching her as little as possible.

Something connected in Christian's mind, and he glanced angrily up at Boleran, dread filling him. "I'm not a lord," he said. "I'm just Mr. Darrow."

Boleran shifted anxiously, glancing to Marie for a moment, then over his shoulder at Christian's father and brother's bodies. "I'm afraid, well, that is to say, you... you're the earl now," he said awkwardly.

Christian swallowed the bile that rose to his throat, but it wasn't enough. He let go of his mother and pushed away from her, rolling to the side and vomiting into the grass. Dear God, he was the Earl of Kilrea. Him, a younger son who was never meant to amount to anything. He'd murdered his father and brother for a title.

"Christian." Marie's voice was soft as she crouched by his side, smoothing her hand across his back. "Christian, this wasn't your fault," she whispered.

"Yes, it was," he groaned, burying his face in the cool grass. "I killed them."

I KISSED AN EARL (AND I LIKE IT)

"You didn't," Marie went on. Christian couldn't tell if she was actually speaking too softly for anyone but him to hear or if his mind was still playing tricks on him. "You didn't mean for this to happen."

"But I did mean for something to happen," he admitted, too ashamed to turn his face to Marie.

"This isn't your fault," she repeated.

He pushed himself to sit, nearly knocking Marie over as he did. She'd hunched close to him. She still held him as he rocked to his haunches, then stood, shaking her off.

"Where is the doctor?" he asked, not looking at her. He couldn't. The guilt was too strong.

"On the way," answered a roughly-dressed man Christian didn't know.

"We should take Lady Kilrea home," Christian heard himself say in a commanding voice he hadn't known he could possess. But after all, he was the earl now. "She shouldn't be here, with this...this...." He dragged his eyes up to stare at the wreckage and his father and brother's bodies, and the driver's beyond. "She should be at home," he finished on a sob.

"Wait until the doctor has come and examined her," Boleran cautioned him. "It's the best chance she has."

"Here he is," someone shouted in the distance. "Here's the doctor."

Christian glanced around, more aware of the scene as the reality of the situation settled around him. A few more carriages had pulled up behind the wreck—probably guests on the way to the engagement party. At least a dozen bystanders stood at the far periphery of the scene, looking horrified and clutching each other. A young woman who seemed to have no place in the middle of such tragedy came forward from the farmer's wagon with homespun cloths of some sort to cover the bodies of his father and brother.

It was too much for Christian to handle all at once. He turned away from everything, burying his face in his hands, and wept.

It was the most painful thing Marie had ever witnessed in her life. Not the splintered wreckage of the carriage or the gruesome sight of Lord Kilrea, Miles, and the driver's bodies. Not the frighteningly injured form of Lady Kilrea. Not even the poor horses that were no longer screaming in pain for reasons Marie didn't want to think about. Watching Christian fall apart as he stood in the midst of unimaginable loss pierced Marie's heart.

"Stand back," Lord Boleran boomed, taking charge of the situation. "Let the doctor through."

Marie had to give the man credit, even if he'd been on the verge of mercilessly marrying his sister off to Christian. He was savvy and compassionate enough to stand with his body shielding Christian from the startled onlookers, giving Christian a shred of privacy as his world fell apart.

Marie looked right past Lord Boleran, reaching

I KISSED AN EARL (AND I LIKE IT)

toward Christian as she started forward. "Christian, it wasn't your fault," she said, or at least started to say.

Lord Boleran caught her by the shoulders before she could come within a few feet of Christian. "Stay back, my lady," he told her.

"But Christian needs me," Marie argued, still too broken by Christian's misery to be offended.

She attempted to step away from Lord Boleran, but he held her fast. "Lord Kilrea needs to speak with the doctor and attend to his mother," he told her.

Anger flared suddenly hotter than pity in Marie's heart. "Let me go this instant," she demanded. "Christian is my—" She snapped her mouth shut over the words. There was no reasonable way for her to complete the sentence. Christian was her lover? Yes, he was now, but admitting as much to Lord Boleran under such circumstances wouldn't just be scandalous, it would be crass.

The doctor reached Christian's side, rested a hand briefly on Christian's arm, and spoke something Marie couldn't hear. Christian sucked in a breath and seemed to pull himself together. He and the doctor rushed to where Lady Kilrea still lay in the billows of her gown. The two men knelt on either side of her, and the doctor went to work.

"Let me go," Marie repeated to Lord Boleran. "I have to see if Lady Kilrea is alive."

Lord Boleran kept his hands firmly in place on Marie's arms but checked over his shoulder as the doctor worked. "She doesn't appear to be dead to me," he said.

"How can you tell?" Marie writhed and twisted, trying to get away from him.

"Believe me, my lady. I've seen death." There was a morbid note to his voice that gave Marie a chill, particularly when he glanced to the other side, where the farm girl who had covered Lord Kilrea and Miles's bodies was now sitting between the two of them, keening as though she were some sort of officially appointed mourn, or perhaps a wise woman charged with seeing their souls to the other side.

"I have to go to him." Marie tried one last time to shake away from Lord Boleran.

"My lady, I'm so sorry, but your fiancé is dead," Lord Boleran said.

Marie blinked and checked anxiously on Christian before she realized Lord Boleran was talking about Miles. She swallowed hard and stopped struggling in his grip. The thought that she had been released from her engagement after all turned her stomach instead of making her feel light, like it should have. But it also made her heart bleed more heavily for Christian.

"Please," she begged Lord Boleran, her voice little more than a wisp. "Let me go."

Lord Boleran sighed and released her. Marie thought about dashing around him and crouching by Christian's side, but Christian's initial bout of grief seemed to have passed. He was stony-faced and grave now—a look that didn't suit him at all—as he spoke with the doctor.

"She's alive," the doctor said, directing the words to

Marie and Lord Boleran. "She has several fractures to her arms and legs, and I fear she may have punctured a lung. There's no way to tell what other internal injuries she's sustained."

"Will she live?" Christian asked, his voice strangely hollow.

The doctor sighed. "I don't know. If there were a hospital nearby, I would urge you to take her there for whatever care they could give. But seeing as the closest hospital is miles away...." He shook his head rather than finishing his sentence. "I'm afraid the journey there would kill her for sure."

"Can we move her back to Kilrea Manor?" Christian asked.

"Carefully," the doctor said.

Marie could do nothing but sit back and watch as Christian, the doctor, and several of the men who had arrived on the scene moved Lady Kilrea to the farmer's wagon. The wagon's bed was cleared and packed with as many cushions and as much straw as could be found so that the journey home would be as painless as possible. Lady Kilrea didn't regain consciousness, and the whole time the men worked to move her to the wagon, Marie feared the woman truly was dead but no one had realized it yet. She tried her best to reach Christian's side, but every time she came close to him, someone pulled her away.

"I'm so sorry for your loss," Lady Aoife said when Marie ended up by her side at the edge of the accident scene. "I know you hadn't yet had time to grow close to Lord Agivey, but he was your fiancé."

It took Marie a few moments to catch up, not only to what Lady Aoife had said, but to the fact that she was there at all. "How...how did you get here?" she asked, too traumatized to think of anything better to say.

"Benedict and I were on our way to the engagement party," Lady Aoife said. "We were within sight of Lord Kilrea's carriage when the driver suddenly lost control.

Marie sucked in a breath so hard at that bit of information that it caused a coughing fit. Lady Aoife slung an arm around Marie's waist and held her carefully. As soon as Marie recovered, she asked, "What happened? Did you see the wreck?"

Lady Aoife bit her lip, looking haunted. "I did."

"What happened?" Marie repeated, pivoting in Lady Aoife's embrace to grab her arms. "Please tell me what happened." Perhaps there was a chance that the carriage hadn't broken apart because of Christian's prank after all. Christian had only loosened a few bolts. Surely, that wasn't enough to cause such catastrophic damage.

"I don't know," Lady Aoife said, tears slipping from her eyes. "They were driving fast. Too fast. Then all at once, there was a twist. The horses broke one way and the carriage looked as though it had been rent in two." She swallowed. "Its occupants went flying in all directions." She finished with a wail, unable to go on.

Just like that, Marie was the one comforting Lady Aoife. It was the last thing she wanted to do, considering

I KISSED AN EARL (AND I LIKE IT)

that more wagons had arrived and men from the nearest village had moved to lift Lord Kilrea and Miles's bodies into another wagon. A second set of men lifted the driver's body to a separate wagon. A few others were taking care of the poor horses as well. Something about the whole thing felt desperate and dire to Marie.

"I need to look at the carriage," she said, not necessarily to Lady Aoife. "I need to see what happened."

She stepped away from Lady Aoife, feeling horrid for doing so, since the poor dear had no one else's shoulder to cry on. But a sense of urgency filled Marie. She had to see the wreckage up close. There had to be a way to prove that the disaster hadn't happened because of the bolts Christian had loosened. The whole thing couldn't be his fault, it just couldn't.

She made it halfway across the expanse of grass separating her from the twisted metal and splintered wood before two men whom she didn't know rushed forward to stop her.

"Stay back, my lady," one of them said. "It could still be dangerous."

"But I have to see," Marie pleaded with them. "I have to check the bolts."

"No, my lady," the other said.

"Yes!" Marie shouted. She began to struggle against them in earnest, shouting, "Unhand me! Let me go!"

"Hush, Marie." The command came from Shannon.

Marie turned, startled to see her oldest sister there at the scene of the wreck. She launched toward Shannon, grabbing her sister's arms as she reached her. "We have to examine the wreckage," she said. "Christian thinks he caused the accident. We have to determine whether his prank is the reason the carriage fell apart. He won't be able to live with himself if it was his fault." Her face crumpled at her last statement as grief swelled within her.

"Christian tampered with the carriage?" Shannon asked, eyes wide.

Marie swallowed hard, then nodded tightly.

"Then perhaps the very last thing we want is to examine the wreckage," Shannon whispered. "If he did cause it, he might be guilty of murder."

Marie thought she might be sick. Of all the ways God could have punished her for the sin of lust and the wickedness of everything she and Christian had done, subjecting Christian to even the whiff of an accusation of murder was the very last thing she expected. What would people say if he really was to blame? Would they accuse him of doing away with his father and brother as a way to gain the Kilrea title? She'd heard Lord Boleran refer to Christian as "my lord" and inform him he was the new earl. Would that alone be enough to raise suspicion?

"No," she whispered, more as a denial of those potential accusations as anything else. She pivoted sharply, searching Christian out. He had climbed into the farmer's wagon and was helping the doctor settle his mother in the nest that had been made for her.

As if he could sense her, he glanced up and met her

eyes. Marie lurched forward, as if she could go to him and somehow make the whole situation better. But the blankness of his expression held her back. He was overwhelmed, beyond feeling anything. She could see that as plainly as if she held him in her arms and the two of them were whispering to each other in bed. All she could do was to put every ounce of the love she felt for him more strongly than ever into her look and nod at him, letting him know she was there for him.

He nodded back, but that was all he could do before the doctor commanded his attention. As soon as he looked away, Marie's heart sank. She couldn't shake the feeling that a terrible wall now divided them.

CHAPTER 7

The terrible feeling in Marie's heart and gut persisted for days. It kept her up nights, tossing and turning and scrambling to remember as many details of the wreck as she could so that she could exonerate Christian. He couldn't have been the cause of the fatal accident, he simply couldn't have. It was just a harmless prank, a bit of fun. Life was supposed to be fun and filled with laughter...wasn't it?

Twined together with her anxiety about the accident was a worry of a different sort. The morning she and Christian had spent together had been magnificent. She'd known full well that she liked Christian, but kissing him so freely and making love to him had been exquisite. His body was every bit as wonderful in action as it had been to look at. Being with him that way had confirmed the one thought that pulsed louder than any other in her mind or her heart. She loved Christian. Yes, the feelings had come on quickly, but she was sure of them. Christian was the only man she wanted to spend the rest of her life with.

He also wasn't replying to the numerous letters she'd sent him in the three days since the accident. Worse still, those letters had come back unopened. That couldn't be his doing, could it? Surely, some servant or solicitor had taken it upon themselves to deflect all of Christian's communications, seeing as he had suddenly been weighted down with the responsibilities of the earldom and his mother's continued dangerous health.

"Good heavens, Marie. You've been holding that spoon halfway to your mouth for so long that I'm surprised your soup hasn't evaporated," Shannon said, snapping Marie out of her thoughts.

Marie blinked rapidly, lowering her spoon and letting it sink in her bowl of soup. She hadn't had much of an appetite for the last few days anyhow. Who could think about food in such a dire situation?

She blinked again when she realized her sisters were all staring at her. Fergus and Henrietta had been invited out to luncheon, which meant the four of them had been left to their own devices for the meal. But instead of laughing uproariously over someone's amusing story or plotting mischief, Marie's sisters were unusually somber. And they were all studying her with varying degrees of worry.

"You've hardly eaten anything since...." Chloe bit her lip, shrugged, and finished simply with, "Since."

"You've hardly spoken either," Colleen said with a far more somber air. "Which is twice as concerning, if you ask me."

"I haven't had much to say," Marie told them, her voice sounding hoarse and unused.

Shannon reached across the corner of the table and covered Marie's hand with her own. "This is a trying time," she said sympathetically, ever the eldest sister. "First, Fergus threw you into an engagement that you didn't want and that was clearly unsuitable for you. Then, your fiancé is killed in an accident."

"Not to mention that Marie was one of the first on the scene," Colleen said with a little too much excitement in her eyes. Colleen always had had a fascination with the morbid.

At the moment, Marie didn't appreciate it at all. "It's not that," she said, her voice dropping to a listless sigh. "I'm terribly worried about Christian."

Her sisters all seemed to freeze for a moment. They exchanged looks that made it clear all three of them knew full well there was much more to the story than they'd been told.

"It's kind of you to be concerned for Lord Kilrea," Shannon said carefully. She eyed Marie closely, as if waiting to see how she would react to Christian being referred to by his new title.

Marie sent her a flat look in return. As much as she enjoyed games and merriment, she wasn't in the mood for anything but the bald truth. "We're lovers," she blurted before she lost the nerve. It was technically true, even if their affair was new.

Her sisters reacted with varying degrees of surprise, and in Chloe's case, delight.

"How exciting and delicious," Chloe said, eyes sparkling. "Is he a good lover? Does he make you feel spectacular? How long does it take to do that anyhow? When do you—"

"Chloe, hush." Shannon silenced her with a stern look. "Now is not the time to interrogate Marie about such things." Her mouth twitched up in one corner. "Though any other time I would encourage every inappropriate question possible, if only as punishment for not telling the rest of us what you intended sooner."

"It happened quite unexpectedly," Marie told them, leaning stiffly back in her chair and fiddling nervously with the edge of her soup bowl.

"I'll say." Colleen stared at her with curious, narrowed eyes. "The two of you only met a month ago."

"I suppose you could say it was love at first sight," Marie sighed, biting her lip and feeling unaccountably sad at the prospect instead of delighted.

"I thought love at first sight only happened in storybooks," Chloe said with a dreamy look, leaning one elbow on the table and resting her chin in her hand.

"If I recall correctly, that first sight involved the sight of his prick," Shannon said, one eyebrow arched.

Marie answered Shannon's stare with a quelling look. "Christian Darrow is more than just a fine prick," she said. "He's a lovely, warm, open-hearted man. Whether we'd known each other one day or one hundred years, it would be the same. We knew at once we were meant for each other." She supposed that was true, looking back on their meeting.

She wriggled uncomfortably in her chair as her sisters continued to stare at her. "And then Fergus had the audacity to engage me to his brother, and Christian's father was mad enough to betroth him to Lady Aoife."

"Both of which were terrible ideas," Shannon said, nodding and gesturing for her to go on.

Marie's face heated, and she couldn't meet her sisters' eyes. "The trouble with being a sensitive, open-hearted man is that Christian was angry over the deal his father made for him. He had a plan to force his father into calling the marriages off. That plan began with a prank that he believed would ensure his father didn't make it to the engagement party." She swallowed hard. "He loosened all the bolts on the underside of his father's carriage."

As expected, all three of her sisters gasped. Shannon looked wary, perhaps remembering the conversation she and Marie had had immediately after the accident.

"He didn't mean to do them any harm," Marie continued with a sudden burst of energy, needing to defend him. "The mischief wasn't supposed to be fatal, and I don't believe it was. I was there when he tampered with the carriage. I saw what he did with my own eyes. I don't believe he did enough to cause the sort of damage I witnessed at the site of the wreck."

"But Lord Kilrea believes he's responsible," Shannon said in a hushed voice.

Marie thanked God that her sister was clever enough to understand the workings of human emotions and guilt. Even so, Marie shook her head and said, "He is *not* responsible. He didn't kill his father and brother. I know it, but he doesn't. I have to find a way to prove to him that the accident wasn't his fault."

"How do you propose to do that?" Shannon asked.

Marie shook her head and shrugged restlessly. "I don't know. I tried to examine the wreckage right after the crash. If I could have just taken a look at the broken axel, checked to see if the bolts were loose or tight and if the breaks happened where everything was fastened together or somewhere else." She felt foolish attempting to explain the construction and workings of the underside of a carriage when, in truth, she didn't know any more about it than she did about the insides of a clock.

A thoughtful look came over Shannon's face. "If everything I've been told was true, Lord Boleran was the first at the scene."

"Yes, he was," Marie said miserably.

"And he stayed behind to supervise the removal of

the bodies and the wreckage of the carriage," Shannon went on.

"He did," Colleen said with an unusually fierce scowl. "At least, that's what I heard." Her cheeks colored suddenly and she avoided her sisters' eyes.

Shannon turned her attention to Colleen. "You have something of an acquaintance with Lord Boleran, do you not?"

Colleen crossed her arms and stared darkly at Shannon. "What are you getting at?"

Marie's interest perked slightly. She hadn't realized there was any sort of connection between Colleen and Lord Boleran. All signs were that there was not only a connection, there was a story.

"Colleen can go to Lord Boleran and ask him what he observed about the carriage," Shannon said, as though the solution were obvious. "With any luck, Lord Boleran will know where the wreckage is now, and Marie can take Lord Kilrea to inspect it."

"I'm not wasting a moment of my day seeking out Lord High and Mighty to ask him about carriage wreckage," Colleen said with a surprising amount of vehemence.

"Not even for the sake of your sister and her handsome and wounded lover?" Chloe asked her with a teasing grin.

Colleen clenched her jaw tightly for a moment, then blew out a breath, letting her arms drop as she did. "Oh, all right," she sighed. "For Marie and for poor Lord

Kilrea. But I won't stay to pass the time of day with the Marquess of Snobsbury."

"Thank you," Marie said, her spirits lifting a bit. "Anything Lord Boleran can tell you that might serve as proof that the carriage wrecked for some reason other than the bolts Christian loosened would be glorious."

"In the meantime," Shannon went on, facing Marie, "you need to eat something before you wither away into a useless slip of nothing. Men don't like to take sticks to their bed."

Marie let out a soft laugh and picked up her soup spoon. Her appetite was well on its way to returning, but she didn't feel completely settled yet.

As soon as luncheon was over and the sisters split to go about their own business, she headed out to the stables, where her bicycle was kept. If Christian wouldn't receive or read her letters, she'd have to speak to him in person, no matter what it took. She mounted her bicycle and sped off down the road toward Kilrea Manor. With a month of practice behind her, she considered herself an expert bicyclist, which meant she had no qualms at all about peddling as fast as the wind, in spite of the fierce glares she received from several people along the road.

She didn't much care to hear about her wicked ways later, though, so as she approached the Kilrea estate, she veered off the main road to take a more discreet, back way to the manor. That path led her along the lush, green valley that divided Christian's property from that of his neighbor, Lord Garvagh. A spring ran the length of the valley, heading toward the sea in the far distance. Close to where it originated, a quaint springhouse had been built. A cluster of trees stood behind the springhouse.

Those trees were where she spotted Lord Garvagh and none other than Lady Aoife. At first, Marie wasn't sure it was them. She was in motion, after all, and at least fifty yards away on the path that cut across the valley on the way up to the manor house. Lord Garvagh was easy enough to make out, with his distinct blond hair and strong build. It was Lady Aoife who came as a surprise to Marie. Though she only had a fleeting glance of the woman as she peddled past, Marie was certain Lady Aoife was in tears, speaking passionately to Lord Garvagh about something.

She only had a minute or so to contemplate the odd scene before huffing and puffing up the hill to the manor's back gardens. All thoughts of Lord Garvagh and Lady Aoife vanished the moment she spotted Christian pacing along the back edge of the garden. Her heart lifted and sank, filling with joy at the sight of him, then sorrow at how miserable Christian looked.

"Christian!" she called out, somehow finding the strength to peddle faster up the last few yards of the hill.

Christian jerked and spun toward her. His expression was grave, but for one, glorious moment, it lifted at the sight of her. All too soon it fell again. He stood still, his shoulders squared in a way that was too stiff and didn't suit him, as Marie rode closer. She had hoped he'd spot her, burst into relief, and run to her, but all he did was wait, his face pinched in misery, as she came to a stop, dismounted and abandoned her bicycle, then rushed toward him.

"Christian," she panted, pressing a hand to her chest as she caught her breath. "I've been so worried about you. I sent you letters, but they were returned."

"I didn't deserve to read them," he said, his voice tired and cracking.

Marie stopped short a few feet from him, blinking in surprise. "So you knew that I sent them? They weren't returned by a servant or...or someone else."

"I returned them," he confessed. Even though he met her gaze firmly, there was something distant and hollow in his eyes, like he wasn't truly there. His eyes were ringed with dark circles, as though he hadn't slept well since the accident. His face was pale and wan, and a layer of dark stubble covered his chin, as though he hadn't had either the time or the will to shave for days. Worst of all, the spark had gone out of his countenance.

"Oh, Christian." Marie surged toward him, throwing her arms around him and hugging him for all she was worth. "I'm so sorry."

He let her hug him, but that was the best that Marie could say. His body was rigid, and even though she couldn't see how it would have been possible in so few days, he felt thinner, diminished somehow. It broke her heart to feel his sadness. No, it went beyond sadness, beyond grief, even. Poor Christian was tortured.

"It wasn't your fault," she said, swaying back but keeping her hands on his arms.

"It was absolutely my fault," he whispered, his voice cracking with guilt and shame. "How could it not be?"

"I swear to you, Christian. I was there with you when you played the prank. You didn't loosen enough bolts or tamper with the carriage enough for it to fly apart the way it did," Marie insisted.

"And how would you know?" He wrenched away from her, his agony turning to anger, another emotion he didn't wear well at all. "What do you know about carriages?"

"Nothing," Marie confessed, letting her arms fall uselessly to her sides. "But I know everything about you, and you aren't capable of murder."

"You don't know anything about me, Marie." The look he sent her was probably meant to be withering, but it missed its mark. She had the innate sense that he was trying to put her off, either to discourage her or punish himself. "We've barely met. We hardly know each other."

"I know more than enough about you to know you could never willfully hurt anyone," Marie said firmly. She wasn't about to let him chase her off.

Apparently, he had yet to catch on to her stubbornness. "You don't know half of the wicked things I've done," he said, taking a step closer to her that was meant to be intimidating. "You don't know the things I did at university or the trouble I got into in Europe with my mates."

I KISSED AN EARL (AND I LIKE IT)

It was the wrong time to laugh, but Marie broke into a pitying smile all the same. "Name a single man who doesn't get up to some sort of wickedness while at university," she said. "Or a young man who doesn't cause more trouble than is good for him while swanning about Europe with his friends." He glanced away, jaw tight, so she went on with, "I doubt a single bit of the mischief you've gotten into in your past is anything other than jolly good fun."

Christian's shoulders slumped a bit more, and he shook his head. "My time for fun is over," he said, bitterness mingling with grief in his voice and expression. "I'm an earl now, or haven't you heard?" He glanced back to her with a look so piteous that it squeezed Marie's heart to the point of pain. "I have an estate to sort out that comes complete with a property dispute. My mother is still in grave danger and hasn't awakened since the accident. And I've a marriage to prepare for." He looked away from her with his last statement, face pinching with despair.

Marie's heart dropped to her feet. "Christian. You cannot tell me that after everything that has passed between the two of us, you intend to go through with your marriage to Lady Aoife." Desperation pulsed through her, making her dizzy.

Christian shrugged. "It was my father's last wish for me," he said in a voice so quiet and melancholy Marie almost couldn't make out his words. "I was such a disappointment to him. The least I can do is obey his last command."

"No, that is not the least you can do," Marie nearly shouted. Christian flinched and glanced toward her. "Marrying a woman you do not love when one who you do love is standing right in front of you is not the proper way to honor your father's memory. Punishing yourself for the rest of your life because you feel responsible for his death is madness, Christian. And besides," her panic subsided a bit as she remembered what she'd seen on the way to the manor, "I believe Lady Aoife is in love with someone else."

Christian frowned at her. "If you're saying that as a way to convince me to change my mind—"

"I'm not. It's true," Marie insisted. "I saw her down at the springhouse with Lord Garvagh just now."

Christian's brow knit together in thought. "What is Ned doing talking to Lady Aoife at the springhouse?"

"Having a secret lovers' rendezvous, no doubt," Marie said, crossing her arms and glaring at him. She was surprised by the amount of sarcasm in her voice and the seemingly poor timing of that sarcasm, but if Christian thought he could just forget what they'd done, he had another think coming. "Lovers' rendezvous? Remember those?" she added for good measure.

Christian turned his head to her, his eyes focusing on hers. For a moment, the flash and the desire were back in his expression. Marie even thought she spotted the corner of his mouth twitching up in a fond grin. The split-

I KISSED AN EARL (AND I LIKE IT)

second reaction faded as quickly as it appeared, though, and Christian shook his head.

"I cannot indulge in childish games and frivolous fantasies anymore," he said. "Father was right. Life is far more serious than that."

"Firstly, I am going to ignore the fact that you just referred to our love as a frivolous fantasy, because I understand you are grieving." Christian glanced away, looking guiltier than ever. "Beyond that, life is only as serious as you make it," Marie argued. "And you, Christian Darrow, were not born to be the sort of man your father was."

"Except that it would seem I am," Christian replied with a helpless shrug. "I wasn't supposed to inherit his title, his land, or his responsibility, but here I am." He held out his arms as if to gesture to everything around them.

"My lord." The call came from a footman who strode purposefully across the garden toward them.

"See?" Christian gestured to the young man, his whole body seeming to sag under the weight of the title.

"My lord, you have a visitor," the footman said.

"I thought I told the staff that I was not at home to visitors today," Christian sighed, walking toward the footman. Marie could do nothing but stand by and watch.

"It's Lord Garvagh," the footman said. "He would like to speak with you on a matter of some urgency. Considering the dispute he had with your father, I thought—"

"Yes, yes, it's all right, Patrick. I'll speak to him," Christian said, gesturing for the footman to go and heading toward the house.

"I'll come with you," Marie said, starting after him.

"No." Christian turned to stop her. Marie pulled up short, her mouth dropping open in protest. "It would be grossly improper for you to be seen at my house," he went on. "Especially since you're not even wearing black." He glanced at her. Heat filled his eyes for a moment, but he forced himself to look away.

Indeed, Marie had boldly chosen not to wear mourning black, even though her fiancé had just been killed. Instead, she wore the darkest green she had, hoping all and sundry would think that was good enough.

"Go home, Marie," Christian called to her as he headed on toward the house. "It isn't right for you to be here. Take your bicycle and ride off to find a man who can love you the way you deserve to be loved."

"But—" Marie stopped herself from protesting as Christian left her. She forced herself to take a deep breath. She loved him, but he was behaving like an arse.

Then again, the man had just lost his father and brother, he could still lose his mother, and he blamed himself thoroughly for the tragedy. In addition to that, he'd had an entire title and everything that went along with it thrown at him when all he'd been expected to do with his life before was enjoy it. The turnabout was so stark for Christian that it was no wonder he wasn't thinking clearly.

She would give him the benefit of the doubt for now, but she wouldn't sit idly by and let him push her out of his life to punish himself. She was more determined than ever to prove to him not only that the accident hadn't been his fault, but that life could still be full of joy and happiness, even after tragedy.

CHAPTER 8

Once, when Christian was stumbling home after a night of carousing with his friends in Rome, he'd stumbled and fallen down a flight of stone stairs. In the process, he'd dislocated his shoulder and had to have one of his other drunken friends push the joint back into his socket. But the pain of that night was nothing to the pain he experienced as he walked away from Marie, knowing he'd hurt her with his coldness.

He hadn't been able to stop thinking about her in the last few days. At least, he hadn't been able to stop thinking about her when his mind cleared enough from the fog of grief and estate business that had settled over him. After his wretched meeting with his father's man of business to bring him up to date on the most dire aspects of his father's dealings, he'd sunken into contemplation of Marie. On his return home from the coroner, after making arrangements for his father and Miles's burials, he'd consoled himself by remembering the way Marie's arms felt around him. All through his consultation with Dr. Phillips about his mother's chances of recovery, he'd contemplated how much easier everything would be if Marie were there to tend to things on his behalf. He thought about how it would be if she were there to tend to him.

Every time his thoughts had turned sweet and flown to her, he'd cursed himself for a fool and forced himself to concentrate. Marie was a beautiful dream that he didn't deserve. Murderers didn't deserve to be happy. And besides, he had a legacy to live up to. He needed to become his father's son.

"That's all bullshit, you know," a voice whispered at the back of his head as he trudged through the garden on his way into the house. "She's right. You're punishing yourself for what happened by keeping her away."

He couldn't hide the truth from himself. But just because he recognized what he was doing and was well aware that he was using Marie—or rather, her absence—as a means of punishing himself, didn't mean he had any intention of stopping. He deserved nothing less than to feel as horrible as it was possible for him to feel.

And yet, underneath all of the tragedy and torture, he could still feel his heart beating. The feeling was faint. The kernel of joy that couldn't be crushed was tiny. But it was there. He would have to destroy it soon, though. Joy had no place in the running of an estate, or in a family that had been decimated by death.

"Oh. Lord Kilrea."

Christian jerked to a stop at the soft, polite exclamation that came from Lady Aoife. She seemed as surprised to see him in the main hallway of his house as he was to see her. The woman's face was as pale and pinched as ever, perhaps more so. A sadness of some sort rimmed her eyes with the slightest bit of red. It was the only hint of color the woman had, either physically or in her spirit. Bless her, but Lady Aoife had always paled in comparison to Marie.

Christian shook himself, forcing his thoughts away from where they wanted to be and focusing on where he should direct them. "Lady Aoife. I had no idea you were here." He approached her gingerly, hands twitching as he debated whether to reach out to her. If she were Marie, he would have folded her in a tight embrace, buried his face against her neck, and breathed in the scent of her as if it were what gave him life. With Lady Aoife, he was afraid to touch her lest she shatter, like a woman made of glass.

"I...I came to inquire about your mother," Lady Aoife said, eyes downcast. She wrung her tiny hands together in front of her—a sign that she was more distraught than she was letting on. Her hands seemed as fragile as the rest of her, and certainly not capable of clasping him close and digging into the muscles of his back, as Marie had during that glorious morning they'd spent together.

Again, he had to force his errant thoughts back to

where they should be. "Have you been up to see Mama yet?" he asked as kindly as he could manage.

Lady Aoife looked up at him as if he'd suggested she descend to the kitchen to help Cook with tea. "I couldn't possibly impose on you in that way, my lord."

Christian smiled tightly. "But, surely, you have a strong connection to this family." He couldn't bring himself to say she would be his wife soon and his mother would be her mother-in-law. He could barely stand to form the thought in his head with her standing right there in front of him, looking like a faded doll instead of the sunburst that was Marie.

"Forgive me," he went on. "I'm being rude. You've come all this way.... Could I offer you tea?"

"Well...er...." She glanced over her shoulder to the parlor. A flush painted her cheeks that had Christian frowning, as though something were going on that he wasn't fully aware of. "If...if you wouldn't mind," she finished in an almost inaudible voice, lowering her head again.

"I don't mind at all," Christian said. "I'm supposed to be meeting Lord Garvagh, but whatever his business is, perhaps he wouldn't mind a lady as lovely as you sitting in on it."

The only reason the compliment was able to pass his lips, the only reason he suggested tea at all and led Lady Aoife toward the parlor was because of what Marie had said. She'd spotted the two of them together by the springhouse, and now here they both were, under his roof. It was as likely as not to be a coincidence. Ned must have been on his way over before and met Lady Aoife on the road. Which was nowhere near the springhouse, but still.

Christian tried to ignore the surge of excitement pulsing through him. He cursed himself for entertaining anything as fanciful and foolish as a secret love affair as he showed Lady Aoife into the parlor. Secret love affairs were jolly good fun, even when they were other people's, but that part of his life was over and done. He was an earl now, and his father's successor. He should be serious, mature, and somber.

But his breath caught in his throat at the way Ned's gaze shot straight to Lady Aoife the moment she entered the room. Hope stirred in him as color actually splashed to Lady Aoife's face, though she kept that face turned away from both him and Ned. He had no right whatsoever to feel the urge to grin at the sudden longing in Ned's eyes, or the way he closed up his expression so fast that Christian felt he should hear the sound of a door slamming to go along with it.

"Garvagh," he said with all the gravitas that the meeting warranted, leaving Lady Aoife to cross the room and shake Ned's hand. "What a pleasure to see you."

"I'm sure it is no pleasure at all," Ned said in his deep bass. "I am so sorry for your loss, Christian. You must know that."

A different kind of hope glimmered in Christian's chest. Ned was the first person to refer to him by his

I KISSED AN EARL (AND I LIKE IT)

given name since the accident. It was a tiny thing, but for the first time in days, it made Christian feel like a man and not a title.

"Thank you, Ned." He returned the favor with as much of a smile as he could manage.

"Your father was a hard man, but a noble one," Ned went on, standing tall and clasping his hands behind his back. For a moment, his gaze flickered to Lady Aoife again.

"Father was Father," Christian said with a wistful look, then quickly said, "I hope you don't mind if Lady Aoife takes tea with us. She's come to inquire after my mother's condition. I felt it would be cruel to send her away with just a short report or to stick her in a separate parlor while we conduct our business." He glanced between the two, keeping an eye out for anything that would support Marie's theory that there was something between the pair.

"How is your mother?" Ned asked, managing to be both compassionate and irritatingly vague about his feelings for Lady Aoife. Other than the initial looks, it was hard to tell if the man even knew she was there.

Christian sighed and rubbed a hand over his face, gesturing for Ned to have a seat on one of the parlor's many chairs. "She's no better than she was yesterday," he confessed. Every thought of romantic undercurrents—or anything enjoyable and diverting—flew from Christian's mind as he glanced to the ceiling and his mother's bed chamber above. "She hasn't awakened since the crash.

Dr. Phillips says she may still be suffering from grievous internal injuries we cannot see."

"They still don't advise moving her to a hospital?" Lady Aoife asked, nodding to the maid who brought a tea tray into the room. Someone must have thought to fix tea for the guests before Christian could come up with the idea.

Christian shook his head. "Dr. Phillips says that as long as she is comfortable and as long as she is able to be fed by the nurses caring for her here, she should stay where she is."

"You know that if there is anything I can do to help," Lady Aoife began, leaving the statement open-ended.

"Thank you." Christian nodded to her, genuinely grateful, but with no intention of asking her to help in any way. He knew beyond a doubt that if Marie had made the same offer, he would have whisked her up to his mother's room immediately and had her take over his mother's care.

That thought was interrupted when Ned cleared his throat. "Christian, I just wanted you to know that, until everything is settled and you are comfortable with your new position in life, I won't press you about this property boundary dispute I had with your father."

Christian's brow lifted in surprise. "I was under the impression that you were adamant about your claims to the land in question. The land your father, and now you, claim is on your property encompasses the spring, does it not?"

"It does," Ned said hesitantly, as if he truly didn't want to talk about the dispute yet. "And as you know, that spring is vital to irrigation for both of our tenant farms, and as a source of drinking water for the tenants."

Christian nodded in understanding, but already his mind was beginning to cloud again with the details. "All I know about the whole thing is that my father was firm in his belief that the land and water rights were ours," he sighed. A headache was beginning to form behind his temples, so he rubbed them. "I'm sorry if I can't recall the details about it off-hand. I'll have to be brought up to speed with Father's man of business. Surely, there has to be a way we can resolve the dispute."

"I'm sure there is," Ned said with a kind smile. He stood. "If you'll excuse me, I truly don't want to impose on you at this time, and it would appear now is not a good time for a social call."

He must have thought Christian had more of a headache than he did. All the same, Christian wasn't sad that the man wanted to leave. He rose as well and shook Ned's hand again. "Thank you for your concern for my mother," he said.

"I should go as well," Lady Aoife said, standing and setting her barely-touched tea aside. She stole a glance at Ned. "Lord Garvagh, would you be so kind as to accompany me to where my brother is waiting for me in the village?"

"But of course, my lady."

Marie was right. Christian was sure of it as they all

said their final goodbyes. But even if Lady Aoife had feelings for Ned and those feelings were returned, what could any of them do about it? Even as part of him argued that the solution was so simple a child could see what should be done next, the part of Christian that was lashed with grief and fuzzy with mourning refused to let go of the idea that he owed it to his father to follow through with his marital plans. He couldn't shake the feeling that marrying his father's choice for him would finally make him worthy in the old man's eyes, even if he was dead. Christian had killed the man, after all. He had an obligation to stick to the plan. That could make everything right.

Couldn't it?

As soon as Ned and Lady Aoife were gone, he flopped onto the sofa beside the table where the tea tray rested. His head pounded more than he wanted to think about, and his heart throbbed achingly along with it. He knew full well that he wasn't thinking straight, that he couldn't think straight, under the circumstances. He wasn't prepared for what lay ahead of him. He hadn't worked his way up to it. Yes, he'd done well at Cambridge. He'd learned enough to get by. But he was an amateur when it came to running an estate and doing what was right for an old family name. But he could still hear his father telling him he was worthless and that he couldn't even stick to a plan as simple as marrying the woman of his choice. Christian would have done just about anything to be able to speak with his mother about

I KISSED AN EARL (AND I LIKE IT)

it. Her opinion would have gone miles toward helping him decide what he should do next.

He had to speak with someone. That truth hit him square in the gut. He might have been an earl and a proud man, but he wasn't so proud that he couldn't seek advice when he needed it. But who was there left to seek advice from? His father was gone. His cousin John was in England. Few other family members remained, and none of them were nearby.

The answer didn't come to him until late that night, as he was crawling, exhausted, into bed. His family was either dead now or scattered to the four winds, but Marie's family was still on hand. Specifically, Marie's brother, Fergus. And while Christian didn't know Fergus O'Shea as well as all that, he trusted the man. Anyone who had endured what Fergus had and came out stronger for it was exactly the sort of person Christian wanted to consult with.

He had to wait until morning, wait until the hour was reasonable to pay a visit to a neighbor. As soon as he could the next day, he washed, dressed, shaved, donned his hat, and made himself presentable enough to pay a call.

It was still embarrassingly early when he showed up on Dunegard Castle's doorstep. It was a good sign that Fergus accepted his call all the same. The man even looked happy to see Christian when a footman showed him into the richly-decorated office deep into the family potion of the house.

"Kilrea," Fergus propelled his chair forward, extending a hand to Christian once he entered the room. "How are you, man?"

"I've been better," Christian said, removing his hat and gripping Fergus's hand. He was more grateful than he would have expected for the strength Fergus showed.

"Understandable." Fergus gestured for Christian to have a seat in one of the leather armchairs in the center of the room. Christian sat, feeling more comfortable once he was on Fergus's level. "I take it there's something I can help you with?" Fergus said, raising the eyebrow over his one eye.

Christian sighed, writhing with second thoughts about letting on that he was anything but prepared for his new life. "I need advice," he said before he could change his mind. "About how to be an earl."

Fergus blinked, inching back in his chair slightly. "That wasn't what I assumed you'd come here for."

Christian had the good sense to look guilty. "You thought I had come to ask about your sister," he said. He wasn't stupid, and he didn't think Fergus was either.

Fergus grinned wistfully. "She hasn't given me a moment's peace about mucking things up with all that engagement nonsense. I'm just so deeply sorry that she had to get her way and get out of the engagement to your brother in the manner she did."

Christian winced. "She didn't get her way entirely," he said, staring at his hat in his hands.

There was a pause before Fergus said, "So you're

going to go through with marrying Lady Aoife? Even though you're a daft fool who is in love with my sister?"

Christian snapped his eyes up to meet Fergus's. "Is it that obvious?"

"Yes, man, it is," Fergus laughed. "The two of you have been shameless since the engagements were announced."

Christian averted his gaze from Fergus. The man had no idea how shameless they'd been. Still, as hard as he'd tried in the last few days, Christian couldn't regret bedding Marie. And he couldn't reconcile the war within him that said he owed more to Marie for ruining her, as was their intent, than he did to Lady Aoife. His heart knew what he should be doing, but his head was still so hopelessly clouded with his father's voice and with guilt. The confusion of the whole thing was maddening. And that was without taking his part in the wreck into consideration. Every which way he turned, every avenue of thought he pursued, was fraught with complications and guilt.

"I don't know what to do," he confessed at last, shrugging helplessly. "I owe so much to so many people so suddenly. I want one thing, but I know I have to accept another. No one prepares you for your entire life being turned upside down in a moment."

"Don't I know it," Fergus laughed, writhing uncomfortably in his chair.

"That's why I've come to you for advice," Christian

rushed on. "You're the only person I can think of who has experienced a reversal of fortune like this."

"I am," Fergus admitted with a grave nod.

"How did you handle it?" Christian leaned forward, setting his hat aside and resting his arms on his knees to stare intently at Fergus. "How did you juggle your responsibilities and your desires? How did you choose between duty and yourself? How could you ever let yourself be happy again?"

The last question tumbled out of him before Christian could stop himself. For Fergus, there probably hadn't been any question of whether he could or should be happy. The attack that had changed his life hadn't been his fault. He hadn't been the one wielding the club. Not like Christian had.

Fergus studied him with a brotherly look and let out a sigh. "There's no way to go on but to take one step at a time. Proverbial steps, mind you," he added with a wry grin, patting one of his legs.

"I'm sorry," Christian said, not entirely sure why. It was the only thing he could say that seemed appropriate these days. He was sorry for the pain of others and sorry for the destruction he'd caused through his own carelessness.

Fergus shrugged. "Part of my life ended," he said. "Another part began. I was lucky to have a good woman standing by my side. Mind you, I tried to run her off. Henrietta wouldn't have it, though. She was far smarter than I was in the end."

A long pause followed. Christian had been staring at his knees as Fergus spoke. When he looked up, he found Fergus staring pointedly at him.

"You have a good woman who's willing to stand by your side too, you know," he said. "And I'm not talking about Lady Aoife."

Shame hit Christian fast and hard. "I don't deserve Marie," he said, aching on the inside. "I don't deserve to be happy, after what I've done."

"Come off it, man," Fergus scoffed. "I understand you're still in shock and you've a great deal more grieving left to do, but only a dolt denies himself—"

Fergus didn't have a chance to finish his scolding. Peals of laughter sounded from the hall outside of the office. A moment later, Marie passed by the doorway with one of her sisters. The two of them were laughing over something. A bolt of joy hit Christian square in the heart, filling him with a burst of longing so acute it squeezed his throat, making any speech impossible. Marie was and always would be the most beautiful, amazing thing he'd ever seen.

But hard on the heels of that moment of light, darkness caved in on him. What right did he have to be happy when his father and brother were dead? What right did Marie have to laugh when the tragedy would swallow up her life too?

Irrational anger lifted him to his feet, and he shot out of Fergus's office, chasing after Marie. Part of him screamed to think twice about what he was doing, but the gaping chasm of sorrow inside of him suddenly seemed to encompass everything. It dragged him under into impulsive desolation before he could stop himself.

"How dare you?" he snapped, grabbing Marie's arm and stopping her in her tracks. She gasped and spun to face him, her eyes wide, but the dam of bitterness that he'd so carefully managed to maintain since the accident burst. "How dare you smile and laugh and pretend as if the world is nothing but a joke when everything has been completely and utterly ruined?"

CHAPTER 9

Marie had never been so shocked in her life. Not only was it a surprise to find Christian in her house too early in the morning for calls, she was startled into silence by the uncharacteristic anger rippling off of him. Everything about him seemed red, from the flush that painted his face to the embroidered accents in his otherwise drab, black waistcoat.

She glanced him up and down, wondering if he was aware of the hint of inappropriate color in the way he was dressed. And he had the nerve to demand why she was smiling?

"There is nothing wrong with me being in a merry mood," she hissed, shaking his hands off of her.

"There is when your fiancé is dead and the man you profess to love is to blame," Christian snapped in return.

He seemed to suddenly notice Colleen a few steps farther down the hall, watching the entire exchange with wide, interested eyes. Marie spotted Fergus wheeling into the doorway of his study.

"What in blazes is going on out here?" Fergus demanded with a frown.

"Nothing," Marie told him. She grabbed Christian's hand and tugged him down the hall. "I need to have a word with Mr. Darrow in private."

"It's Lord Kilrea now, and it is highly inappropriate for the two of us to be given any sort of privacy whatsoever," Christian grumbled, letting Marie lead him down the hall to a drab parlor that was rarely used all the same.

"Do you see my brother trying to stop us?" Marie asked over her shoulder, one eyebrow arched. "Or my sister for that matter?" She immediately answered her own question with. "No. And they won't. Because they can see as clearly as I can that you, Christian Darrow, need a stern talking to."

She pulled him all the way into the stuffy parlor then turned to face him, arms crossed. Christian's mouth fell open, and he gaped at her as though she'd grown another head. "My entire world has fallen apart, and you're treating me like a disobedient child?"

"Your entire world has fallen apart," Marie repeated. "That is why I didn't slap you on the spot and run you out of the house while poking you in your backside with a fire iron."

She couldn't maintain her irritation or continue on with sharp words. Not when Christian's shoulders fell as though he carried the weight of the Matterhorn. He let out a heavy breath and scrubbed a hand across his face. With the initial bout of emotion between them over, she could see how exhausted Christian was. Dark circles still rimmed his eyes. His dark, curly hair was more unruly than usual. His eyes still held little more than pain and regret. It was as though Marie were looking at a badly-drawn image of him instead of the real Christian.

She took a cautious step toward him, resting a hand on his back, then rubbing it. "How is your mother today?" she asked, hoping it was a topic that would defuse his obviously raw emotions.

"The same," Christian admitted in a small voice. "She has yet to awaken, but she appears to be resting comfortably. She is able to swallow the broth that the nurse feeds her, even though she isn't conscious of it."

"That's something," Marie said. She shifted to stand facing him fully, risking a slight smile. "Do you want to know why I was smiling and laughing just now?" she asked.

Christian's brow darkened, which wasn't at all the reaction Marie was hoping for. "Have you pulled some sort of jolly prank on one of your sisters? Did you find another naked man on the beach, and did you convince the locals he was a merman this time?"

Marie pursed her lips. "You're an arse when you're upset," she said. "But I tell you, to me, that only proves that you're not as crushed by everything that happened as you say you are."

"I am devastated," he croaked. For a moment, Marie

thought he would burst into tears, as shocking and unmanly as that would have been.

"Devastated, but not defeated," she told him, keeping her back straight and her chin up. If Christian didn't have strength of his own at the moment, she would need to be strong for both of them. "You wouldn't be snapping about like a Nile crocodile or shouting at me if you didn't have life left within you."

He gaped at her. "Of all the cruel things to say when my father and brother have had their lives dashed out of them due to my fecklessness."

Marie took a deep breath before going on. Christian's pain and guilt were raw, and she had the feeling it would take a monumental effort to bring him out of both.

"The carriage accident was not your fault," she said, pulse racing with the information Colleen had discovered late the day before.

"Please, Marie, don't." Christian rubbed a hand over his face again. "I need to come to terms with—"

"The bolts on the carriage's axel were as tight as could be," Marie interrupted him.

Christian's mouth continued to hang open for a minute as he stared at her. "How do you know?"

"Lord Boleran told Colleen as much yesterday," Marie said, breaking into a smile. "That's why I was smiling and laughing. Colleen hates the man, but she called on him to ask about his impressions of the wreck. We both saw that he was the first one on the scene, and he took charge of disposing of the wreckage afterwards.

He told Colleen that there was nothing at all wrong with the bolts."

"Why did that cause you to laugh?" he asked.

"I wasn't laughing at the accident, I was laughing at the way Colleen was making a complete ninny of herself by grousing about Lord Boleran."

For a moment, Christian continued to stare at her. Hope lit his expression. He shook it away far too soon, turning from Marie. "He must not have looked carefully enough. What else could cause a wreck so destructive? He must have looked at the axel wrong."

"Would you rather believe that? Do you *want* yourself to be at fault somehow?" Marie crossed her arms again. "Or will you see the truth of things and accept that accidents happen?"

"I should have been a better son," Christian whipped back toward her. "I should have obeyed my father without question and without hesitation."

"By marrying a woman you don't love and living the rest of your life in misery?" Marie challenged him.

"You don't understand." He turned away again. "Sons have a duty toward their fathers."

"Yes, and now your duty is to manage his estate to the best of your ability and to live a life full of joy, since he and your brother cannot live that life anymore."

"I can't just be happy," he started, turning back to her. His mouth worked to finish the thought, but no further words came out. "I can't just be happy," he repeated, making the words a single thought.

"You can," Marie told him. "Death is a horrible thing, especially when it comes unexpectedly. But the only way to fight against death and to win is to live to the fullest in every moment you are given. You cannot bring your father and brother back, but you can honor them by enjoying every second you are given."

"No." He shook his head, then swallowed hard and started toward the hall. "I don't deserve to be happy ever again."

"Christian." Marie chased after him, but the moment he reached the hallway, he strode swiftly toward the door. Fergus's butler was ready and waiting for him and held the door so that Christian could escape out into the rainy morning.

Marie let out a breath and shook her head. Grief was never an easy thing. She'd experienced it twice before, when each of her parents died. Time was the only thing that cured grief, but she was afraid time was something Christian wasn't willing to wait for. Not with his engagement to Lady Aoife still in place, nor with the shock of responsibility now heaped on him.

"My lady." Marie was startled out of her thoughts as the butler left the door after closing it behind Christian and strode down the long hall toward her. He glanced into the formal parlor as he passed it, then met Marie's eyes as he continued on. "My lady, you have guests in the formal parlor."

Marie blinked, wariness prickling its way down her back. "Guests? So early?"

"Lord Boleran and his sister, my lady," the butler reported.

Marie's brow rose even higher. It seemed as though her thoughts of Lady Aoife had summoned the woman. "Thank you, Mr. Connelly," she said stepping past him and heading toward the parlor.

A conversation was already underway between Lord Boleran and Shannon, but Marie caught the last of it as Shannon said, "He came to call on my brother, no doubt for advice about the running of his estate."

A strange twist filled Marie's stomach as she nodded politely to Lady Aoife and headed for one of the empty chairs. Halfway across the room, she changed her mind and went to sit on the sofa beside Lady Aoife instead.

"He could have come to me for advice," Lord Boleran told Shannon with a slight frown. "He's to be my brother-in-law soon."

"And why would anyone in their right mind ask your advice about anything?" Colleen snapped. She was glaring daggers at Lord Boleran, which made Marie wonder what sort of exchange they'd already had.

Lord Boleran appeared to be exercising extreme patience as he turned to Colleen and fixed her with a stern scowl. "I happen to have rescued my father's estate from the edge of ruin when I inherited it five years ago, my lady," he said through a clenched jaw.

"Rescued it, you say?" Colleen huffed as though that were impossible. "Was the estate stuck up a tree, like a cat?"

"Colleen," Shannon warned her with a frown.

Chloe had a hand to her mouth in order to hide her giggling.

Colleen didn't seem to notice either. "Do you fancy yourself a hero, Lord Boleran?"

Lord Boleran's back was stiff as he replied, "I fancy myself a man of vision who takes his responsibilities seriously."

"Very seriously, I'm sure," Colleen said in a scathing voice.

Marie shifted her gaze back and forth between the two of them, increasingly baffled. She knew that Colleen had unusually strong feelings for the marquess. She was aware that the two of them had encountered each other on more than one occasion, at balls and local fetes and the like. But she'd had no idea that whatever connection existed between them could elicit the sort of sparks that flew between them now. Whether Colleen was aware of it or not, those sparks weren't entirely adversarial.

"Please let me express my condolences for your loss yet again, Lady Marie," Lady Aoife spoke softly at Marie's side, almost as though she intended to start a side conversation while the others talked about their own business. No other conversation began, though, so Lady Aoife was forced to speak with everyone listening to her. "If you are in need of proper mourning attire, I could give you the name of my seamstress in Ballymena."

Marie fought down a surge of irritation and picked at the forest green skirt she wore. "Thank you, my lady, but my hope is that this old gown is sufficient for mourning a fiancé I barely knew."

Lady Aoife's pale face splashed with pink, and she looked away.

Marie didn't try to hide her wince. "I'm sorry, Lady Aoife. I didn't mean to snap." She reached for Lady Aoife's hand to squeeze it. "I know that your condolences are genuine. And you are right. I should don proper mourning attire because of my connection to the family."

Lady Aoife seemed to forgive her. She lifted her face timidly to Marie and smiled. "It's just that I feel responsible," she said in a whisper.

Marie wanted to smirk at the word. "Responsible" was becoming a theme she couldn't escape.

The others fell into a conversation about the rain, which gave Marie a chance to speak to Lady Aoife in relative privacy.

"Responsible?" Marie asked. Part of her hoped to draw the woman out. She couldn't forget what she'd seen by the springhouse the day before.

"Because I'm...I'm to be the Countess of Kilrea soon," Lady Aoife said, lowering her head and looking as miserable as if her fiancé was the one who had died.

Marie's heart thrummed with paradoxical excitement. "And this isn't something you want?" she asked cautiously. If she could get Lady Aoife to admit she was in love with Lord Garvagh, there was a chance she could have Christian—or even Lord Boleran—call the engagement off.

"What I want isn't important," Lady Aoife said, glancing wistfully toward one of the parlor's rain-streaked windows.

A thrill of triumph shot through Marie's gut. Lady Aoife obviously didn't want to marry Christian. Discovering that was the first step toward untangling the rest of the mess.

"I would think that your feelings on matters of love are highly important." Marie still held the woman's hand. She patted it, then clasped it in both of hers, showing as much warmth and friendship as she could.

"Marriage and love do not always go hand in hand," Lady Aoife said, dragging her eyes reluctantly back to Marie.

"But they should." Marie stared intently at her. She had to wring an admission from the woman, but she had to do it delicately. "You don't love Lord Kilrea." She phrased her question as a statement, hoping it would be easier for Lady Aoife to admit to it that way.

"I'm certain I will grow to love him in time," Lady Aoife said.

Marie took a deep breath to battle her frustration with the woman's answers. "He is a lovely man," she said slowly. "But perhaps not the loveliest of your acquaintance?"

A sudden, guilty look drew all color out of Lady Aoife's face. "Whether I find any man lovelier than the man I have been told I am to marry is irrelevant," she said, barely audible.

"But there is someone?" Marie practically vibrated with impatience. Why could the woman not just own up to her true feelings and take what she wanted?

Because women had been schooled for centuries to do as they were told and accept every sort of meddling in their lives, she answered herself. Because up until very recently, a woman's feelings weren't considered important at all, particularly not where marriage was concerned. Marie was beyond grateful that the mindset which had given birth to those horrible ideas was changing, even if it wasn't changing fast enough.

"I will do as my brother tells me," Lady Aoife said, evidently not willing to stand up for herself like a modern woman.

Frustration had Marie ready to leap out of her skin. How were women ever supposed to rise up to take their rightful place in the world when so many continued to see themselves as unworthy of something as simple as demanding to marry whomever they pleased?

"You'll do as your brother says, even if it means you'll be unhappy?" Marie asked subtly. She leaned closer to Lady Aoife. "Even if that means some other, worthier gentleman will be made unhappy by the decision as well?"

The look Lady Aoife gave her in response to the suggestion reminded Marie of a rabbit that had been cornered by a fox and knew it was about to be devoured. "I...I cannot imagine what you mean by that, Lady Marie," she stammered.

The other conversation in the room stumbled to a halt, and all eyes turned to Marie and Lady Aoife. Which was no surprise to Marie. Lady Aoife looked as guilty as sin and ready to burst into tears.

"Aoife, are you well?" Lord Boleran asked, standing and putting aside the teacup he'd been holding. "Perhaps we should return home so that you can rest. My sister has a delicate constitution," he said to Shannon by way of apology.

"Anyone who is forced to endure your presence on a daily basis would have a delicate constitution," Colleen muttered, tilting her nose up.

Marie sent Colleen a scathing look and stood as Lady Aoife did. "If there is anything I can do to help you in any way, my lady," she said. "If you ever need a friend to confide in, someone who might have been a sister to you."

Lady Aoife smiled weakly at her, but rushed away as soon as her brother swept her from the room.

The next few minutes were spent bidding farewell to the guests. Marie bristled with frustration, even as she smiled and curtsied and pretended nothing was wrong. The moment Lady Aoife and Lord Boleran were gone, though, her sisters rounded on her.

"Whatever did you say to make Lady Aoife blanche so?" Chloe asked, as though she were asking Marie for the plot twist in the novel she was reading.

"She looked terrified enough to faint," Shannon said with a far more pointed stare.

Marie returned to the sofa, flopping into it. "Everything is a muddle," she said as her sisters sat around her.

"What sort of a muddle?" Colleen asked.

"A matrimonial muddle." Marie sighed, then sat straighter. "Christian believes he's still obligated to marry Lady Aoife, because it was his father's last wish for him, even though he's in love with me."

"Oh," Chloe said with a rapturous smile. "Did he confess that love for you? Was it glorious and romantic?"

"He did not confess it in so many words," Marie said, feeling as though she'd missed out on what was her due, "but it's true. And Lady Aoife still feels obligated to marry him, even though she's in love with someone else as well."

At that revelation, both Chloe and Colleen gasped.

"Who is Lady Aoife in love with?" Colleen asked.

"Lord Garvagh," Marie said. "I spotted the two of them in an intimate conversation yesterday while on my way to call on Christian." She tilted her head to the side, remembering the way Lady Aoife had looked as though she were in tears. "I think she's as miserable about being forced to marry Christian as Christian is over what he thinks is his part in the accident."

"But he didn't cause the accident," Colleen said. "Benedict might be a complete arse, but he knows of what he speaks when it comes to carriage wreckage."

Marie, Shannon, and Chloe all turned to Colleen, and all three of them managed to ask in unison, "Benedict?"

Colleen's face flushed puce. "Lord Boleran." She cleared her throat. After a split-second of guilt, she burst into anger. "Oh, never you mind. You have your secrets and I have mine. But before you chastise me, I hate the man, and nothing half as wicked as what Marie and Lord Kilrea did has happened between the two of us."

"But you wish it would," Chloe said, then dissolved into giggling snorts.

The sisterly exchange was enough to send bursts of light through Marie's whole body. Everything had changed, and yet some things would always remain the same. Her sisters were a steady force that she could always rely on. They were bold, brave, and powerful when it came to determining their own futures.

She would be bold and brave too.

"I am not going to sit idly by and let four people's lives be ruined by this foolish marriage," she said, standing. "Lady Aoife is in love with Lord Garvagh. I am in love with Christian. If it's the last thing I do, I am going to see that the right people marry each other, even if I have to break a hundred carriages to do so."

"Perhaps that isn't the right analogy for the time," Shannon said in a scolding voice.

Marie's cheeks heated. "Perhaps not, but my intention is the same. I am going to make things right, and I am going to start by convincing Christian that he deserves just as much love as any other man and all the happiness life can provide him."

CHAPTER 10

Unlike a large number of men of his acquaintance, Christian had never shied away from emotions, even intense ones. But as he sat beside his mother's bed, brushing her face lightly with a damp cloth to clean away the last traces of the broth the nurse had fed her for supper, he wondered if men who eschewed emotion had the right idea after all. His heart twisted in his chest at the sight of his proud, strong mother looking so frail. Her dark hair was streaked with grey and fanned out over the pillow, and her skin was pale and papery as she slumbered on. There had been a few encouraging signs that day, moments when it had almost seemed like she would awaken, but they'd come to naught.

The ache he felt at seeing how old and helpless his mother had become was nothing to the half dozen or more kinds of guilt he felt, though. The days-old guilt that lashed him over his part in the accident still throbbed deep in his chest, but newer, sharper forms of shame skated over top of that now. He shouldn't have shouted at Marie that morning. She was only trying to help him. He'd been too consumed with grief to allow that the world around him was still moving and happiness still existed. He felt guilty for experiencing a moment or two of that happiness. Being close to Marie had warmed parts of him that had frozen over. He felt horrible for wanting more of that, wanting her. Which made him miserable, because he still believed he had a duty to marry Lady Aoife. Except, he now questioned whether he really had that duty or if it was just an echo of the way his father had always lashed out at him for being a terrible son. He didn't want to spend the rest of his life haunted by his father's ghost, but a large part of him still craved the man's approval.

"I don't know what to do, Mama," he whispered, putting the damp cloth aside and taking his mother's thin hand in both of his. "I just want to do the right thing, but it's become so muddled. I don't know what the right thing is anymore."

No answer came from his mother's prone form, but somehow Christian knew that his mother was full of advice, and that she wanted nothing more than to be able to give it to him. He longed painfully for the moment when he could hold his mother in his arms and the two of them could weep together over the loss of the other half of their family. Even if his father and Miles hadn't been open or loving with either him or his mother throughout their lives, they were still family, and they were still gone.

"My lord, if you don't mind, I'd like to settle Lady Kilrea for the night," the nurse spoke behind Christian.

Christian drew in a breath and stood. "Yes, of course. Thank you, Nurse Brannaugh."

He bent to kiss his mother's cheek, closing his eyes and saying a quick prayer for her, then straightened and backed away. For a few moments, he stood near the doorway, watching the nurse tend to his mother, but the sight pierced him with even more guilt. His actions were what had landed his mother in the state she was in now, after all.

He gave up watching and turned to leave, striding down the hall toward his bedroom in the other wing of the house. As he walked, he unbuttoned his jacket and waistcoat, loosened his tie, and tugged his shirt out of his trousers. By the time he reached his own room, shut the door, locked behind him, and lit a lamp, all it took was a few quick movements to toss his clothes aside. He sat in the chair by the empty fireplace to remove his shoes, then kicked off his trousers and drawers as well.

Once naked, he stood and crossed to his bedside table, where a half-empty bottle of whiskey from the night before still sat. He grabbed it and pulled out the cork with his teeth—like he used to do with any wine or spirits bottle that reached his hands while carousing his way through Europe—and tossed the cork on the table. He took a long draught that seared his throat and made him cough before wondering whether drowning his sorrows was really the best idea. At least the whiskey warmed his insides, which had felt numb since the accident.

He took one more swig before setting the bottle down and crossing back through his room to pick up the clothes he'd carelessly shed. There was no point in making more work for the poor sod who'd decided to be his valet. He didn't need a valet, but Gordon had worked for his father for years, and Christian felt yet another shade of guilt over the idea of sacking the man.

He'd gathered all of his clothes and tossed them into a hamper in his wardrobe when a sharp knocking made him jerk and whip toward the door, his brow shooting up. The knocking hadn't come from the door, though. After a second knock, he whipped the other way, only to discover it'd come from the window.

It was dark and dreary outside, and he'd only lit the one lamp. Even so, he could clearly make out the form of Marie on the other side of one of his bedroom windows. He gaped at her as he hurried across the room to unlatch the window and thrust it up.

"What in God's name are you doing, woman? And how did you get up here?" he demanded. His heart ricocheted around his chest, and he couldn't decide if he was happy to see her, shocked that she was at his window, or furious with her for being there in the first place.

"My, my," she said, her wide eyes sweeping his naked

form. "You do like to walk about in the altogether, don't you, Lord Kilrea?"

The urge to laugh bubbled up in him so quickly that the effort to suppress that laughter made him dizzy. "A gentleman can walk about naked in his own bedroom," he said, then rushed on to, "How did you know which room was mine, and for God's sake, what are you doing on that ladder?"

"You're answering your own questions, you know," Marie told him, pushing him back and climbing up the last few rungs of the ladder that she'd brought from heaven only knew where to reach his window.

She hoisted her leg gracelessly over his windowsill and pulled herself into the room. At the same time that she reached for him, probably to steady herself, Christian stepped back, intent on giving her the room she needed to climb in. The result was that she lost her balance with a muffled shriek and tumbled to the floor, arms and legs sprawled. She groaned, though Christian couldn't tell if it was from embarrassment or injury.

"What sort of hellion brings a ladder to an earl's house and climbs through his window in the middle of the night?" Christian asked, finding her shoulders in the tangle of skirts and limbs and hefting her to her feet.

"A wicked one," Marie answered, meeting his eyes with a fiery look. "And it's not the middle of the night. It's barely ten o'clock. There are parties throughout the county that are only just beginning at this hour."

"Parties you should be attending rather than being

here." Christian knew that he should turn her around and push her toward the window so she could climb out again and be on her way. At the very least, he should take his hands off her and step back. He couldn't seem to do either, though. All he could manage was to hold her and rake her with a gaze.

She returned that assessing, head-to-toe gaze, and she had far more to look at than he did. Her mouth twitched up in one corner. "You truly are the nakedest man I've ever known," she said.

"What are you doing here, Marie?" he asked before her mischievous humor could trick him out of all the guilt and sorrow he should rightfully be feeling.

"I'm here to save several lives," she said with a triumphant grin. For a moment, she rested her hands on his arms, then moved them to his sides, then quickly slid them to his chest, leaving tendrils of desire pulsing through him. A heartbeat after that, she pulled her hands away entirely and stepped away from him. "I've no idea where to put my hands, and I cannot think at all with them anywhere on your body," she said, deliberately turning to one side. "I cannot look at you either." As soon as she said that, she cheated her eyes back to him, focusing on his cock—which wasn't as flaccid as it should have been. "Strike that. I cannot help *but* look at you," she went on, her lips twitching into a saucy grin. A grin that she instantly stifled. "No, it's best if I avert my eyes."

She turned fully away from him.

"You still haven't told me what you're doing here,"

Christian said. He put on as stern an expression as he could manage, but his heart overflowed and excited energy coursed through him, whether he wanted it to or not. He considered going to his wardrobe to fetch a robe, but stubborn pride kept him glued to his spot. At least, he hoped it was stubborn pride and not a far cheekier sort of satisfaction that came from knowing she liked the look of him. Or that he enjoyed how it felt to have her look.

Marie tensed for a moment before letting that tension out with a breath as she turned to him. "You cannot marry Lady Aoife. She doesn't love you. She loves Lord Garvagh instead. And you love me." She paused, but before he could launch into an explanation of why none of that mattered, she added, "And I love you."

Those words hit him far harder than Christian anticipated. Marie loved him. Of course, he knew she loved him, but to hear her say it, plainly and honestly, was like an arrow piercing his heart. Except, instead of taking his life away, that arrow infused him with life and purpose.

He didn't dare entertain those feelings, though.

"Love is inconvenient at the moment," he said, gesturing helplessly. He must have looked especially helpless, saying as much while stark naked and on display for her. "I'm terribly sorry that Lady Aoife's heart longs for someone else, but—"

"Don't you dare tell me you have to marry the poor woman anyhow, just because your father wanted it," Marie rode over him, taking a hard step toward him. The intensity of her glower was enough to shock Christian right out of the certainties that he knew to be true. "I can account for your confused thinking because you are grieving, but if you persist in marrying the woman, knowing she's in love with Lord Garvagh and you are in love with me, then you're a bigger fool than I thought it was possible for you to be."

He wanted to argue with her. He wanted to spout volumes about duty and honor, his father, family legacies, and so on. Except that he didn't. He didn't want to argue at all. He didn't want to marry Lady Aoife, he wanted to marry Marie. He wanted it so badly that it made every fiber of his being burn.

With paradoxical coolness that he didn't truly feel, he asked, "What am I supposed to do about it? The betrothal has already been made."

"We aren't living in some medieval society, where oaths are bound in blood and where wars are started because of broken engagements, Christian," Marie told him, crossing her arms and shaking her head. "You are the most dramatic man I've ever met. Nudity, pranks, wallowing in sorrow."

"I love you, Marie, but I'm not going to stand here and listen to you mock me like this," Christian replied.

A sudden, wide grin split Marie's face. Her eyes danced like leaves in the summer breeze and her cheeks went as pink as the sunrise. "You love me," she said. It was a repetition of his own words, but it was a way of calling him out as well. "I knew it," she went on, tilting her chin up haughtily. "I knew that underneath all that hurt your heart was still beating."

She was still mocking him, but that didn't mean she was wrong. The shell of grief and horror that had closed in around him after the accident began to crack and break away, letting the sunshine of the love he felt for her peek through.

It would have been so easy to give in to that love. The man he'd been a week ago would have thrown himself headlong into it. But he'd changed in the last week. He'd grown up, and he had to take responsibility for himself and others.

"Are you absolutely certain that Lady Aoife is in love with Lord Garvagh?" he asked seriously, stepping toward her. Only a few inches separated them, but he restrained himself from reaching for her.

"I am as certain of it as I can be," she said, equally serious. "I tried to get her to confess this morning, but she wouldn't let go of what I suppose is loyalty to you. Or perhaps to her brother, whose wish it is that you marry. Though heaven only knows why the man is so determined to see his sister wed."

Christian frowned. "That's not enough to make a decision this important. It's not enough evidence to break an engagement."

Marie let out a sigh of frustration that was almost comical in its intensity. "Are you still so stubborn that you're demanding proof of Lady Aoife's love?"

"Yes," Christian answered with a shrug. On the one hand, he couldn't, in good conscience, go against what his father and Lord Boleran had set up. On the other, seeing Marie aggravated and ready to tear into him lit a fire inside of him that he'd sorely missed. He wanted to feel again, desire again, and she was well on her way to granting that wish.

"Fine," Marie huffed, either not seeing how she was affecting him or enjoying the game as much as he was beginning to. "We'll prove that Lady Aoife and Lord Garvagh are in love and that everyone would be much happier if they were allowed to marry."

"How?" Christian planted his hands on his hips, secretly hoping the gesture would draw Marie's attention to his quickly-growing arousal.

"We'll play a prank on them," she said. "So to speak. We'll find a way to get the two of them alone together and...." Her words faded as her gaze dropped to his groin. Her already pink cheeks grew redder, and her eyes sparkled with hunger. A naughty smile spread across her lips, and she bit one, as if contemplating how she could take a bite out of him.

Christian cleared his throat, his pulse kicking up.

Marie drew in a breath and forced her eyes to meet his. "Sorry. What was I saying?"

"Something about getting two lovers alone," Christian said, grinning. Lord help him, he was actually grinning. For what felt like the first time in years.

Marie met that grin, fire flickering in her eyes. "That's right. We get Lady Aoife and Lord Garvagh alone. In...in the springhouse." Her expression brightened with an entirely different kind of mischief. She paced to one side. "We come up with a way to trap them in the springhouse. That way, they'll be forced to confess their love for each other."

"Forced," Christian repeated with a mock serious nod. He loved watching the gears turn in Marie's brain, loved watching her get carried away on the wings of a mad-capped scheme. It made him want to run away with her. It made him want to be happy.

"Once they confess their love, it should be easy for you to break the engagement," she went on before stopping her pacing and her explanation with a gasp. "I know! Oh, Christian, it's pure brilliance."

"Yes, it is," he said, admiring the light that seemed to surround her. He paused, then said, "What is?"

She strode toward him, closing the distance between them. "This is more than a way to unite Lady Aoife and Lord Garvagh in true love. This is a way to resolve your property dispute as well."

For a moment Christian frowned. "It is?"

"Yes." Marie clasped his arms, sending spears of fire through him that settled in his groin. "Don't you see? You can offer Lord Garvagh Lady Aoife's hand in marriage in exchange for the property rights your families have been disputing for so long."

Christian arched one eyebrow doubtfully. "Now who's being the medieval one? Brides are not bartered for land anymore."

"I know, but my guess is that Lord Garvagh will be so grateful to you for releasing Lady Aoife from her engagement that he'll give you whatever you want."

"Will you give me whatever I want?" he asked. The question surprised him, and for a moment, they both blinked in shock.

Then Marie let out a breath and shifted her arms to rest over his shoulders. "Oh, yes, Christian. I will give you whatever you want and then some."

She surged into him, slanting her mouth over his. Every reasonable voice within him said he should push her off, cast her aside, and go about life the way a serious, stoic gentleman in the midst of an incalculable loss should. For a change, he didn't listen to a single one of those voices. He wanted Marie wrapped around him. He wanted her under him. He wanted to be inside of her. He wanted her in his life forever.

He kissed her back, not caring about anything else but the sweet taste of her mouth and the way her tongue tangled with his when he thrust his into her. She accepted him with a moan of longing that sizzled through his blood and had him hard in seconds. Her fingers combed through his hair as he fumbled for the fastenings of her skirts and whatever other parts of her he could reach to undress her as quickly as possible.

"I love you, Marie," he said between desperate kisses. "I love you more than I know."

He wasn't sure if his words made sense. What did make sense was the way her skin felt against his as they

I KISSED AN EARL (AND I LIKE IT)

worked together to remove her clothes and move to his bed.

"You can make fun of me for enjoying nudity as much as you want," he panted as he unclasped her corset while she fumbled awkwardly to unlace her boots—two actions he wouldn't have thought were possible at the same time. "But you must admit, it's a damned sight more convenient than all these clothes."

"I'll never wear clothes again," Marie vowed as they tangled and flopped their way through undressing her.

It was madness—so much that he found himself laughing as one of her boots got stuck in his bedcovers before she could remove it and as her chemise ripped when he tried to pull it over her head. Undressing was chaos, but they managed to accomplish enough of it to slide their bodies together with absolute bliss.

"Oh, God, this feels so good," she sighed as he stroked his hands along her sides and nibbled at her neck.

"So good," he echoed, grinding his erection against her hip.

He wanted to touch her everywhere at once. He wanted every part of his body in contact with every part of hers. He cupped one of her breasts and brought his mouth down to suckle her nipple, eliciting sounds from her that had his balls drawn up tight with expectation. She tasted of salt and wonder, and the way she wriggled under him as he teased her to greater heights of pleasure was better than anything he'd ever experienced before. He switched to her other breast, rolling her abandoned nipple between his fingers and thumb as he suckled the other, then pinched lightly.

Her response was electric. She cried out wordlessly, arching into him. He didn't know how he was going to hold out long enough not to embarrass himself with his lack of control. Her response to the way he kissed across the flat of her stomach and explored between her legs left him hot and throbbing.

"Christian," she panted his name as he pushed her thighs apart and kissed the inside of first one, then the other. "That's...that's...ohh!"

He drew a deep cry out of her as he explored her with his lips and tongue. She was so eager for him that he had to grip her thighs tightly and hold them apart so that he could tease her clitoris with his tongue. Something told him that she liked the way he handled her forcefully as much as she enjoyed what his lips and tongue were doing. That something resolved into a deep gasp and a cry as her body convulsed in orgasm at his touch.

It was the most beautiful thing he'd ever experienced, and he wanted to experience all of it. He repositioned himself as fast as he could, thrusting into her with a satisfied cry, then holding himself within her for a moment. The sensation of her inner muscles squeezing and milking him was too much to resist. He moved decisively within her, feeling his control shatter with lightning speed. All he wanted to do was be one with her, now and always. All his heart longed for was to spill himself inside of her and to feel whole again.

He came with a thunderous jolt of pleasure, his whole focus narrowing into the pleasure that coursed through them both as he emptied himself inside of her. It was magical beyond telling, filling him with life and joy. The feelings were so wildly perfect that as soon as the bliss of orgasm began to subside, he lost every last ounce of energy he'd been holding onto and collapsed half on top of her.

"I love you so," she panted, embracing him with her arms and legs and sighing in contentment. "You are mine, and don't you ever forget it."

"I won't," he promised hazily, already feeling the weight of sleep descend on him.

And there was another shade of guilt he hadn't yet experienced. He was a cad for falling asleep minutes after coming inside of her. But for the first time in days, his heart and soul felt light. For the first time, he felt safe, as though everything would be all right after all. It wasn't an insult to her that he drifted off quickly, it was the greatest compliment he could possibly give.

CHAPTER 11

Marie had won. She knew it as certainly as she knew she loved the sound of Christian's deep, sated breathing as he slumbered after making love to her. She knew it like she knew that, come what may, the two of them would be together for the rest of their lives and all of eternity beyond. She could feel that the spell of grief that had trapped Christian in its web was breaking and that he would soon be thinking like himself again.

She also knew that there was still work to be done.

She woke Christian briefly, deep into the night, whispering to him that she had to return home before anyone suspected anything, but to have Lord Garvagh in place by the springhouse early the next afternoon. Christian was still so exhausted that all he did was hum and nod and let her kiss him soundly—then kiss him again when that kiss proved to not be enough—then tiptoed back to his window and climbed down to where her bicycle was waiting. She'd let Christian's servants discover the ladder against the window the next morning and think what they would. Perhaps a new hint of scandal would be just the thing she needed to push Christian over the edge into chasing his own matrimonial desires instead of sticking to his father's ridiculous idea of a match.

By sheer force of luck, Marie was able to return home and sneak up to her bedroom in the wee hours of the night without anyone spotting her. She tried to sleep once she was home free, but her mind wouldn't let her. It turned over her plans to force Lady Aoife and Lord Garvagh together, and once she was certain her plot was fool-proof, it buzzed on with ideas for how she and Christian could be married as soon as possible, in spite of the strictures of mourning that Christian was obligated to observe for his father and brother. When she finally did fall asleep as the first rays of dawn were peeking over the horizon, it was with a smile on her face.

"Did you enjoy your lie-in?" Shannon asked late the next morning, a knowing grin pulling at her mouth, when Marie joined her sisters in their family parlor.

"I did," Marie answered with a happy sigh.

"I'm sure she especially enjoyed the lying part," Colleen added with a smirk, stabbing a needle into the embroidery she was working on.

Marie didn't even try to pretend her sisters had the wrong way of things. "If you'll excuse me," she said after striding across the room to pluck a scone from the tea tray sitting on a table between Shannon and Chloe. "I have a very important call to make."

"Let me venture a guess," Shannon said. "Are you about to grace Lord Kilrea with your company?" She arched one eyebrow.

"I'd wager she already did that and more last night," Colleen muttered.

Marie's sisters exchanged looks that dissolved into mischievous giggles.

"For your information," Marie said, biting into her scone, then chewing to heighten the expectation of the moment. She hadn't realized how hungry she was or how good the scone would be, but she went on regardless with, "I am paying a call on Lady Aoife."

"How curious," Shannon said, looking as though she genuinely meant it. She darted a look to Colleen, then said, "Be sure to pay your respects to her brother on Colleen's behalf while you're there."

"You will not!" Colleen snapped, face flushing.

"If you do, tell me everything about how Lord Boleran looked when you gave him Colleen's regards," Chloe said, stars in her eyes.

"You will do no such thing," Colleen nearly shouted.

"I doubt I'll have time to see Lord Boleran at all," Marie said, finishing her scone as she strode across the room to the door. "Although I have it on good authority someone will need to pay a call on him later today to explain why his sister's engagement has been called off." She flickered her eyebrows cunningly.

I KISSED AN EARL (AND I LIKE IT)

Shannon sat straighter with an impish glint in her eyes. "Good heavens, you aren't thinking of running off with Lady Aoife yourself, are you?"

Marie laughed at her sister's teasing and headed out to the hall. If she had her way, Lord Garvagh would do the running off with Lady Aoife before the afternoon was over.

It took no time at all for her to fetch her bicycle from the stables and to ride the handful of miles to Boleran Hall. By the time she reached the grand and modern estate, it was lunchtime. The day was unusually sunny and bright, and as it had the added advantage of being balmy, Marie wasn't surprised at all to find Lady Aoife taking her luncheon outside on a lovely patio that stood in the middle of a well-tended rose garden. The sky was a vibrant blue, the grass around the garden was vivid in its shades of green, and the roses burst forth in every color from red to coral to yellow, sending the most delicious scents into the air. The only colorless, drab thing in the picture was Lady Aoife herself.

"Lady Marie, this is a surprise," Lady Aoife said, rising uneasily from her luncheon table and adjusting her black skirts so that not a wrinkle showed. "Have you... have you come to dine with me?" The poor woman looked genuinely flabbergasted and disturbed by Marie's presence. Though that might have had something to do with the letter that lay open on the table beside her plate. She snatched it up and folded it hastily, tucking it into the waistband of her skirt.

"I've not come to dine," Marie said, feigning an air of urgency that was part of her plan. That act faltered for a moment as she glanced across the deliciously pink ham and herb-sprinkled vegetables on Lady Aoife's plate. Her stomach growled, but there was no time to stop and eat. She took a step toward Lady Aoife, reaching for her hands. "Lady Aoife, my dear friend. I need you to come with me at once."

"Come with you?" Lady Aoife blinked rapidly, her face coloring. "Is something the matter? Is it…is it Lady Kilrea?"

Marie had planned to use a different excuse—one involving a puppy in need of help—but if Lady Aoife wanted to write her own script for the prank, then Marie would go along with it.

"Yes," she said. "You must come with me to Kilrea Manor at once."

"Of course." Lady Aoife stepped away from her lunch, following Marie quickly and willingly as they crossed through the rose garden to the side of the house where Marie had left her bicycle. "Has she expired?" Lady Aoife asked, her voice high and tight. "Or has she recovered?"

"There's no time to lose," Marie said, hurrying on.

"Should I prepare myself? How is Lord Kilrea faring?" Lady Aoife wrung her hands, looking genuinely distressed.

Marie frowned over the woman's concern. It was ridiculous for her to think she was the only one who had a right to worry about Christian, but she allowed herself that bit of ridiculousness. Christian was hers, and soon the world would know it. "You'll see," she said.

"Should I have a carriage brought around? Should I inform my brother that things have taken a turn?"

They reached the side of the house and Marie's bicycle. Frustration got the best of her. Of all the times for Lady Aoife to suddenly start talking and asking questions.

"We'll take my bicycle," she said, grabbing the handlebars and pulling it around to point toward the drive.

"Both of us?" Lady Aoife balked. Of course she would.

"Yes. You can ride on the handlebars."

For a moment, Marie thought Lady Aoife's eyes would pop clean out of her head. "How is that even possible?"

"It's easy," Marie told her. "I rode on the handlebars last week while Christian peddled."

Her careless remark earned a look of shock and suspicion from Lady Aoife. A light of understanding came into the woman's eyes, but before she could come close to saying anything about it, Marie growled and said, "Hurry. Time is wasting. It's a simple matter of climbing up, sitting here—" she patted the cross-section of the handlebars, "—and keeping your skirts out of the way."

Lady Aoife didn't look at all convinced, but she followed Marie's instructions and climbed onto the handlebars all the same. As it turned out, it was neither simple nor easy to ride a bicycle with someone sitting on the handlebars. Christian must have been some sort of miracle worker to make it look as easy as he had. It took Lady Aoife several attempts to balance and Marie several more to propel the bicycle forward before they were on their way down the drive.

Even then, the journey proved a thousand times more arduous than Marie had accounted for. Every time she peddled fast enough to help balance the bicycle and its load, Lady Aoife began to scream in panic. In doing so, she shifted her weight on the handlebar, making Marie fight to maintain balance and momentum. They nearly crashed four times, but Marie was fiercely determined to keep going.

In the end, the difficulty of the ride aided the overall deception Marie had planned.

"That's it. We cannot go on like this," she panted with genuine frustration as they reached a portion of the road that was within sight of the springhouse. "I need to rest."

"I don't think I could go on either," Lady Aoife agreed, pressing a shaking hand to her chest as she slipped off the handlebars and staggered to one side.

Marie scrambled for something to say, scanning the area around the springhouse to see if Christian had followed through with his part in the deception. She nearly shouted for joy when she spotted him and Lord Garvagh striding toward the springhouse from a hill closer to Lord Garvagh's property. Her relief was quickly eclipsed by alarm, though. Lady Aoife couldn't see Lord Garvagh before they were ready to spring the trap.

"Good Lord, have you ripped your skirt?" she asked, nudging Lady Aoife to turn so that her back was toward the springhouse and the men.

"I don't think so," Lady Aoife said. "I was sure to be careful and held my skirts as close as I could."

"I'm certain I heard a tear, though." Marie bent to grab the hem of Lady Aoife's skirt, then proceeded to check every inch of the fabric of both the skirt and the petticoat underneath.

She plucked and fussed and did whatever she could to keep Lady Aoife distracted. When she had the woman vexed to the point of madness, Marie glanced toward the springhouse. She was just in time to see Christian open the door and invite Lord Garvagh to enter ahead of him. Christian glanced in Marie's direction as he did, but the distance was too great for Marie to see what sort of expression he wore.

Once Christian followed Lord Garvagh into the springhouse and shut the door behind them, Marie stepped away from Lady Aoife. "I must have been mistaken," she said. She wiped her brow with the back of her hand. "Would you mind if we stopped at the springhouse for a drink of cool water? I could use it."

"Yes, I believe I could use some refreshment as well," Lady Aoife said, fanning herself, lips pursed. "As long as it won't delay us from reaching Lady Kilrea's bedside as swiftly as possible."

"It won't," Marie lied. She picked up her bicycle from where she'd let it drop by the side of the road and wheeled it toward the nearest stand of bushes. "I think I'll just leave Lucifer here for the moment."

"Lucifer?" Lady Aoife's brow shot up in alarm. "I was riding on a contraption named Lucifer?"

"It's a fitting name, no?" Marie teased her as they walked through the grass following the path of the spring.

Lady Aoife didn't answer. Or rather, her wary, sideways look was all the answer Marie needed.

The closer they drew to the springhouse, the more anxious Marie grew about her plan. As she'd detailed it to Christian briefly before leaving him the night before, they would trap Lady Aoife and Lord Garvagh in the old stone structure together for as long as it took them to declare their love. The details of that plan, however, were sketchy at best, now that Marie was faced with the moment of truth. Getting Lady Aoife to enter the springhouse might not be that hard, but getting Christian out without being seen, so that Lady Aoife and Lord Garvagh could be alone and believe they were not being spied upon was another entirely.

There didn't seem to be any way to proceed but to charge on once they reached the springhouse.

"Oh, dear." Marie stopped within a few yards of the door. "My lace seems to have come loose." She crouched and pretended to fiddle with her boot. "Go on

I KISSED AN EARL (AND I LIKE IT)

in without me." She gestured for Lady Aoife to proceed.

To Marie's surprise, Lady Aoife only hesitated for a moment before shaking her head as though she were supremely perturbed and pulling open the springhouse door.

Marie held her breath, waiting and hoping everything would go to plan, as Lady Aoife stepped over the threshold.

"Oh! Ned! What are you doing here?" Lady Aoife's voice sounded from the echoing inside of the old building.

At the same time, Christian popped his head around the edge of the stone wall. His expression was neutral and his face was still paler than it should have been, but his eyes sparkled with curiosity.

That was all the provocation Marie needed. She leapt into action, lunging for the springhouse door and shutting it with a loud thunk. "Oh, no!" she called out with as much feigned distress as she could. "I seem to have stumbled into the door. I think it's wedged shut."

Marie gestured for Christian. He sped forward, joining her at the door and throwing his weight against it. When someone on the other side tried to push it open, Christian held it shut.

"It does appear to be stuck," Lord Garvagh said. "Let me try—"

Christian and Marie both braced themselves hard against the door as Lord Garvagh attempted to throw his own weight into it. The blow Lord Garvagh delivered to the door was bruising. Marie hoped and prayed that she and Christian together would be strong enough to keep it shut.

"Stand back a moment," Marie called through to their prisoners. "Let me see if I can just get this to...." She let her words fade and gestured for Christian to fetch the wedges she'd asked him to bring to keep the door stuck tight.

Thankfully, Christian had grasped what she intended for the prank. He darted to the side and took four sturdy wedges that he'd evidently placed around the corner of the building earlier. As he fetched them, Marie noticed his trousers were soaked from the knees down.

"If I could just—" Marie pretended to be studying the door as Christian pounded the first wedge into place at the bottom of the door. "It just needs a little—" He followed by securing two more wedges between the side of the door and its frame. "Perhaps a bit of—" Finally, he finished by knocking the last wedge into place at the top of the door. "There," Marie said. "Try now."

She and Christian stood back, holding their breaths. Christian reached for Marie's hand, grasping it tightly. A moment later, a hard thump sounded from the other side of the door as Lord Garvagh threw his weight into it. He tried a second time, then a third. The door didn't budge.

"Whatever you've done seems to have made it worse, Lady Marie," Lord Garvagh's grumbling voice said.

I KISSED AN EARL (AND I LIKE IT)

"Oh, dear," Marie said with a smile as broad as the ocean.

"Whatever are we going to do?" Lady Aoife asked.

"Lady Marie, you must find Lord Kilrea at once," Lord Garvagh commanded. "He was here minutes ago. He climbed down through the spring door with the intent of showing me a feature he has plans to install, but he seems to have disappeared."

"How very odd," Marie said, sending Christian an impish grin.

Surprisingly, Christian met her wicked look with a smile of his own. It was weaker than what she felt it could be, but after days in which the only expression she'd seen on Christian's face was misery—or transportation, as she'd seen briefly the night before—the expression and the light it brought to him were priceless.

"Hurry," Lord Garvagh charged her. "Lady Aoife is greatly distressed."

"And we cannot have that," Marie said under her breath, sending a victorious look to Christian. "I'll run as fast as I can," she called into the springhouse. "In the meantime, are you certain you'll be all right completely alone, without a soul nearby to hear you, unchaperoned?"

Christian swatted at her arm, as though he thought she was laying it on too thick.

"We'll manage," Lord Garvagh said. There was an intimacy to his tone that had Marie's pulse racing in victory.

"All right. I'm going now," Marie called out.

Still holding Christian's hand, she moved away from the door. Rather than leaving to head up to the manor house, she and Christian walked around the corner to the side of the building where the spring ran down from the hill. The spring sank underground several yards away from the building, which meant a flat patch of grass stretched along that side. It was the perfect place for Marie and Christian to stand with their backs pressed against the stone wall, listening to whatever conversation would happen inside through the thin and patchy roof.

It took a few seconds in which all they could hear was movement from inside the building before Lady Aoife sighed and said, "How long are we going to be trapped here?"

"It shouldn't be long," Lord Garvagh told her. "Lord Kilrea only just left, moments before you arrived."

"I'm surprised the man isn't more concerned about where you've gone," Marie whispered to Christian.

"I believe he has other concerns at the moment," Christian whispered back.

"Aoife, there's no need to look so distressed," Lord Garvagh went on in a tender voice. "We won't be trapped here for long. Even if the door is stuck, we could still climb out through the spring door below, or through the roof." There was a pause in which Marie could just make out the sound of Lord Garvagh walking across the creaking floorboards inside the building. "I'd no idea the roof was in such dire need of repair."

"At least it lets the light in," Lady Aoife said in a tremulous voice.

More creaking followed, then Lord Garvagh said, "I mean it, Aoife. There's nothing to be afraid of. I'm here. I'll keep you safe."

"But don't you understand, Ned, this is a sign." Judging by the slightly muffled sound of Lady Aoife's words, Marie was convinced Lord Garvagh had embraced her. She sent a triumphant look to Christian, whose entire countenance was filling with mirth as the scene played out. "This is a punishment."

"A punishment for what, love?" Lord Garvagh asked in the most tender voice Marie had ever heard from the man.

"For loving where we shouldn't," Lady Aoife went on. "For disobeying my brother and wishing things were other than they are."

"Your loyalty to your brother is admirable, sweetling," Lord Garvagh said, "but as I've told you so many times before, it is misplaced. Benedict was wrong to betroth you to a man you do not love when a man who does love you is right here."

"Oh, Ned."

"I wish you'd let me tell him I was the one he saw creeping out of the crofter's cottage that night," Lord Garvagh went on. Marie's brow shot up. "Then this whole tangle wouldn't have happened."

"I couldn't bear it if he harmed you, Ned." Lady

Aoife's plaintive words were followed by a heavy stillness and the faintest sounds of movement.

Marie turned to Christian, eyes wide, barely able to suppress her laughter. "They're kissing," she mouthed, pointing at the wall.

Instead of smiling and laughing along with her, Christian's face crumpled into sorrow and defeat. He slumped against the wall, scrubbing his hands over his face.

Marie shifted to stand in front of him, her feet braced on either side of his. "What's wrong?" she whispered, taking his hands away from his face.

"I've been such an idiot," Christian admitted in a hushed voice. "You tried to tell me those two were in love and I was too blinded by grief to listen. You tried to tell me a lot of things."

"This isn't right," Lady Aoife said with a burst of energy inside the spring house. "We shouldn't be doing this."

"Yes, we should," Lord Garvagh insisted. Marie was fairly certain Lady Aoife had tried to pull away and he'd stopped her, perhaps even pulled her back into his arms. "I love you, Aoife. I am the only man who has a right to marry you."

Marie planted her hands against the wall on either side of Christian's shoulders. She arched one eyebrow and nodded to the building, as if seconding what Lord Garvagh had said for herself where Christian was concerned.

"We've waited far too long to declare ourselves," Lord Garvagh went on. "If we'd been bold enough to tell the world what we wanted from the beginning, we wouldn't be in this bind."

"If I'd put my foot down when my father insisted I marry her," Christian echoed, resting his hands on Marie's waist.

"It's not too late," Marie told him.

"But look at the mess we're in now," Lady Aoife said. "We've defied duty, and now look. We're trapped in here."

"Only for the time being," Lord Garvagh said.

"But so much tragedy has occurred," Lady Aoife insisted. "I cannot help but believe old Lord Kilrea and Lord Agivey's deaths are divine retribution for the night of passion we spent together."

Marie's brow shot up so fast that it made her dizzy. She pressed her lips tightly shut to keep from bursting with laughter. It seemed she wasn't the only wicked woman in County Antrim after all. She never would have guessed Lady Aoife had it in her.

Christian's expression was still pained, though, and his shoulders slumped.

Marie opened her mouth to speak, but miraculously, Lord Garvagh beat her to it by saying, "God doesn't punish us for love. Or for disobedience about something as small as ill-advised betrothals. The divine wants us to be happy in all things."

"But the accident," Lady Aoife tried to go on.

"Accidents happen," Lord Garvagh said. "They just do. Without any rhyme or reason. They aren't meted out as punishment for our sins. They are unfortunate coincidences, and we cannot throw away any chance we have for happiness because the world is an imperfect place. Daring to be happy in the face of tragedy is what gives life its meaning."

Marie clasped the sides of Christian's face as Lord Garvagh spoke, staring intensely into Christian's eyes. Her heart echoed every word Lord Garvagh spoke and then some.

"It was not your fault," she whispered, tears stinging at her eyes as emotion rushed in on Christian like a hurricane.

Christian nodded. It was a tiny movement, all things considered, but it carried within it a surrender that seemed to set Christian free. His eyes were still filled with grief and his face pinched with a fresh wave of pain, but everything else about him felt lighter, lifted up.

The extended silence from inside the springhouse hinted to Marie that Lady Aoife and Lord Garvagh were kissing again, and she'd be damned if they were the only ones. She leaned into Christian, slanting her mouth over his and pouring her heart and soul into kissing him. His arms surrounded her at once, his hands spreading across her back. He straightened, strength rushing back into him as he caressed her mouth with his and explored her with his lips and tongue. If Lord Garvagh kissed Lady Aoife half as passionately as Christian kissed her, the entire springhouse might burn down.

"I love you," Christian whispered as he rained light kisses across her cheeks and chin. Marie tilted her head back so that he could nip and lick her neck. "I love you so much, Marie. I'm sorry I even considered marrying someone else."

"I knew you would never go through with it," Marie replied, eager to have his mouth on hers again. "And I know you've been grieving. So it's easy to forgive you."

"I'm sorry all the same," he said. They stopped trying to keep their voices down.

Marie pulled away from him, taking a step back. She briefly registered something not right about the grass under her feet, but that was the least of her worries at the moment. "It's all over now," she said, grasping his hand as if to pull him away from the springhouse wall and taking another step back. "Let's let them out of the trap and get everyone engaged to who they're supposed to be engaged to." She flickered one eyebrow. "And then we can go up to the house and—"

She didn't have a chance to finish her sentence. As she took another step back, a loud crack sounded under her, and the ground gave way, plunging her downward.

CHAPTER 12

Christian grasped and scrambled, but he wasn't fast enough to maintain his grip on Marie's hand as she plunged into what seemed like a hole in the ground. She screamed sharply, but a hollow splash quickly drowned out the sound.

"Marie!" Christian started forward, but wheeled back when another crack sounded and the ground under him tilted. He leapt to the side in time to avoid tumbling into the spring as another section of the ground collapsed.

In a flash, he realized what had happened. The spring didn't simply disappear into the ground before entering the springhouse. Someone had built a deep channel to direct the water and covered it with floorboards of some sort. Only, the construction had been done so long ago that grass had grown up over the boards. If enough time had passed since that had happened, it was as like as not that the boards had rotted. So when

I KISSED AN EARL (AND I LIKE IT)

Marie put her full weight on them, they gave out, plunging her into the stream.

All of those thoughts happened in a split second. Christian twisted as soon as he hit solid ground beside the collapsed section of boards and grass, scrambling to the dank chasm that had been uncovered.

"Marie!" he shouted louder, desperate to find any trace of her. There was no telling how deep the spring was at that point or what sort of debris might be trapping Marie underwater.

"Kilrea, is that you?" Ned's voice boomed inside the springhouse.

Christian barely registered his question. "Marie's fallen into the spring," he called out, tearing away whatever boards he could get his hands on in an effort to reach her. The boards were so rotted that they crumbled in his hands rather than giving him splinters.

Banging sounded from inside the springhouse, but Christian hardly heard it.

"Christian!" Marie's watery, strangled cry came from somewhere far below.

"I've got you, Marie," he called to her, doubling his efforts to move boards and rend the earth to reach her.

"Christian, I can't hold on," Marie cried back. The fear in her voice had the hair on the back of Christian's neck standing up.

"I've got you," he repeated, though his heart trembled with uncertainty.

He tried to think fast, tried to remember what he

knew of the springhouse and what he'd seen just minutes before. If Marie let go of whatever she was holding onto, would she sail right underneath the structure and come out the other side, or were there gratings or other obstructions that would trap her underwater?

A loud crack split the air, and a moment later, Ned and Lady Aoife dashed around the corner of the springhouse. Ned leapt right over the gaping hold left by the broken boards and dropped to a crouch on the other side.

"What happened? Did she fall through?" Ned asked.

Christian nodded, giving Ned only a cursory look. "The boards gave out," he said, pulling more away.

"Can I help?" Lady Aoife asked, moving forward and heading toward a section of the grass that Christian expected hid more unstable boards.

"Stand back, love," Ned warned her sharply, then bent to tear at the old boards with Christian.

"I'm slipping," Marie gasped below them. "It's all wet and slippery, and—oh!"

Christian tore aside just the right board and spotted her in the nick of time. He lunged for her, closing a hand around her wrist and pulling for all he was worth.

A moment later, Ned managed to grab hold of Marie's other wrist. Between the two of them, they yanked her free of the cold spring water, the mud, and the dark. Ned let go once Marie's head and shoulders were above ground, and Christian tugged her the rest of the way out of the hole and into his arms. The two of them tumbled back onto the grass together. Marie's skirts were sodden and thick with mud, and she shook violently as Christian closed his arms around her.

"It's all right," Christian panted, stroking his hands over her back, arms, shoulders, and finally her face, both to make certain she was truly all right and to comfort her. "I've got you. Nothing is going to hurt you now."

"Christian."

His name was the only word she was able to get out before he kissed her. Perhaps he shouldn't have been so ardent with Ned and the woman who was technically still his fiancée looking on, but he couldn't help himself. He kissed Marie with all the passion and relief he could manage, sighing and stroking every part of her that he could as the pure joy of having her alive washed over him. He was so overcome that he rolled her to her back and covered her, continuing to kiss her lips, her cheek, her neck and any part of her he could, even though she was muddy and musty.

"Marie, I love you," he said between kisses. "I love you, I love you, I love you. I'm never letting you out of my sight again."

Marie laughed wildly, but didn't manage to form whatever wicked thoughts she had into words before he captured her mouth in another kiss.

It was only after Christian had nearly exhausted himself with relief that he became aware of Ned and Lady Aoife standing together, only a few yards away. The impropriety of their situation hit him then, and he shifted off of Marie, struggling to stand. He offered Marie his hand and helped her to stand as well.

"Are you well, Lady Marie?" Ned asked, a curious look on his face. The man's mouth twitched, almost as if he were trying not to smile.

"I...." Marie ran a hand through her wet, mud-streaked hair, then patted her arms and body, as if trying to determine the answer. "Miraculously, I think I'm well after all that," she said with a weak laugh.

A moment later, her face pinched with guilt.

"I'm so sorry, Lord Garvagh, Lady Aoife," she blurted. "Christian and I trapped you in the springhouse deliberately in an effort to get you to admit your feelings for each other. I knew you couldn't possibly marry Christian," she told Lady Aoife, her words fast and breathless. It was as if Marie suddenly needed to confess absolutely everything as penance after her brush with death. "I know you love Lord Garvagh, and I love Christian." She leaned into Christian, grasping his hand. "None of us would have been happy if we'd gone through with what the idiots who arranged our betrothals wanted."

"But...but how did you know?" Lady Aoife blinked rapidly, blushing harder than Christian had ever seen a woman blush.

"I saw you with Lord Garvagh right here the other day," Marie confessed. "But I'd noticed the way the two of you look at each other before that."

"You are observant, Lady Marie," Ned said, continuing to look as though he might want to smile, but didn't dare to.

Lady Aoife gasped suddenly, clasping a hand to her chest. "Dear God, you heard me confess to...to...." She squeezed her eyes shut, as if doing so could block out everything they'd heard her say to Ned in the springhouse.

"You're not the only one," Christian told Ned, hoping the man would catch which way the wind was blowing so that further explanations weren't necessary.

"That was the reason my brother was so adamant about engaging me to whatever gentleman he could," Lady Aoife said. "He knew I'd sinned, and he feared the consequences. He...he demanded I reveal my lover's name, and when I refused to incriminate Ned, he arranged a marriage he believed would be suitable. But Ned is the man I love."

"Lord Kilrea," Ned said with exaggerated formality, standing straighter. "I would humbly request that you break your engagement to Lady Aoife." He stepped closer to the woman's side, slipping an arm around her waist. "I believe Lady Marie is correct in that we would all be happier if we were able to follow our hearts and not our misguided senses of duty."

"I agree," Christian said. The spark of a thought kept him from shaking hands on everything yet, though. "I agree on one condition," he went on.

"Condition?" Marie gaped at him, looking ready to browbeat him if she didn't like what he said next.

A grin pulled at the corner of Christian's mouth. "As I understand it, in medieval times, brides were traded for land." He peeked at Marie. "A wise scholar suggested that the practice could be renewed."

Ned's back stiffened, and he narrowed his eyes at Christian. "Are you saying you'll only release Lady Aoife to marry me if I give over this disputed property to you?"

Christian could see at once that driving that hard of a bargain would hurt him in the long run instead of helping. "No," he said with a laugh. "I was just teasing. But I do think the two of us should be able to come out to some sort of agreement that will allow for shared rights to the spring and its benefits. Are you willing to compromise for a deal that will benefit all?"

Ned smiled, extending his hand. "I am," he said. When Christian shook the offered hand, Ned went on with, "You're a far better negotiator than your father ever was. I have a feeling we've entered a new era of cooperation between our estates."

His words were meant as a compliment, but they squeezed Christian's heart with almost unimaginable sorrow. "My father," he said, glancing off into the distance. The grief that had held him in its grip threatened to drag him under again, like the flow of the stream had almost dragged Marie to a watery death.

Before those thoughts could truly take hold, though, he spotted one of his footmen racing down the hill toward them. "My lord!" the young man called, his voice as

I KISSED AN EARL (AND I LIKE IT)

urgent as his running. "My lord, you must come now. Your mother!"

Christian didn't wait to ask what the man meant by his words. He shot into motion. Marie ran with him, in spite of her sodden clothes. Even Ned and Lady Aoife raced up the hillside toward the house with him.

"My lord, she's awake," the footman gasped as Christian and Marie reached him.

"Awake?" Marie panted.

"Yes, my lady." The footman glanced briefly to Marie as they all dashed for the house. He went on with, "And she's asking for you, my lord."

Christian was wet from his thighs down, caked with mud, and smelled of sweat and stagnant water, but he didn't care. He tore through the house—Marie keeping close to his side, even though she was more of a sloppy, dripping mess than he was—and up the stairs to his mother's bedchamber.

A cry of joy nearly ripped from his lungs as he burst into her doorway, only to find his mother sitting up in bed. The sling encasing her broken left arm was more visible with her sitting up. Dozens of pillows were propped behind her, and she still looked as weak as a baby bird as a nurse fed her broth, but she was clearly awake.

"Christian," she choked out, raising her shaky hands to him.

The nurse pulled away as Christian charged to his mother's side.

"Mama," he groaned, practically throwing himself into her arms, as though he were still a lad of five. She was and always would be his mother, and he needed her right then more than he'd ever needed anyone. "Oh, Mama, you're back." He wept against her shoulder, not caring who saw him so unmanned.

"There, there, dear," she said in a wisp of a voice. "You're all right, my darling."

Christian poured his heart out in weeping for a few more seconds before the fullness of the situation hit him. He jerked straight, grasping his mother's thin, cool hands, and looked guiltily into her eyes. "Mama, did they tell you what happened?" he asked, his voice cracking.

His mother nodded, her face pinching and tears forming in her eyes. The way her soft lips quivered and grief filled her face was too much for Christian to bear. But he had to bear it. Responsibility wasn't only about solving property disputes and marrying the right woman, it was about being the rock that the people he loved needed in their darkest moments. Marie had taught him that.

"I'm so sorry, Mama," he said, trying to be strong. Tears streamed across his cheeks all the same. "It was my fault. The accident was all my fault. I...I killed them."

His mother's eyes widened, and her mouth quivered for a moment before she could ask, "What do you mean?"

Christian shook his head, sniffing wetly and wiping his eyes with the back of his hand. "I was angry at Father for engaging me to Lady Aoife without my consent.

Marie is the woman I love, and I was determined to do whatever it took to get out of one marriage so that I could marry her."

"That did not kill your father, a carriage wreck did," his mother said. With a supreme effort of will, she raised her good hand to pat his head.

"But the wreck was my fault." Christian forced himself to go on. "I thought that if Father was unable to reach the engagement party, it would buy me more time to get out of the betrothal. So I...I loosened the bolts on the axel of Father's favorite carriage so that it would break down on the way to Dunegard Castle." He lowered his head in absolute shame.

"Oh, my dear, sweet, foolish boy. We discovered the problem with the bolts before we got into your father's preferred carriage," his mother said. Christian snapped his head up at her revelation. "Morris knew something was wrong with that one and had already determined we should use the other carriage. And so we did."

"You were riding in another carriage that day?" The idea had never crossed Christian's mind. Nor had he thought to visit the carriage house to see whether the carriage he'd tampered with was still there. He felt like the biggest fool imaginable. But he also felt free.

"It was a hare," his mother said, shaking her head and squeezing her eyes shut. "I saw it dart across the road and was in the middle of noting its speed to your father when the horses reared. Seconds later, it happened. I don't remember anything after that."

"Spooked horses could cause that kind of an accident," Marie said in a gentle voice, stepping closer to Christian. She had hope in her eyes, as though something she had known all along had finally been proven true. Christian loved her more than ever for it.

"Good heavens, Lady Marie?" his mother said, sagging back against her pillows. She was losing strength. Christian wanted to leave her to sleep and recover, but his mother's gaze was fixed on Marie. "Oh, my dear, I have done you such a great disservice."

"You've done nothing of the sort, Lady Kilrea," Marie said, coming forward, but stopping short of sitting on the bed or reaching out in her current state.

His mother shook her head and squeezed her eyes shut. "I should have stood up to my husband when he suggested you marry Miles and dear Lady Aoife marry Christian. I could see as clear as day from the moment I first saw the two of you together that you were meant for each other and no one else."

"You could?" Christian blinked, his heart feeling lighter and lighter with each new revelation.

"A blind beggar could see that the two of you are best suited for each other," his mother went on, her voice growing softer as her strength waned. "Who else would be able to keep the two of you rapscallions in line but each other?"

Marie laughed, then clapped her hands to her face. Her eyes grew glassy with tears.

"I should have forced your father to renege on the marriage arrangements," his mother said.

"There's no need to worry, Mama." Christian stood, leaning close to kiss his mother's forehead. "Everything has worked out well in the end. I'm no longer engaged to Lady Aoife." And Marie clearly wasn't betrothed to Miles any longer. "You need to rest and build up your strength."

"Yes, yes I must be strong for the wedding," his mother said, her eyes closed.

"Mama, I just said there would be no wedding. Lady Aoife and I have agreed to end our engagement."

"Not that one," his mother said, managing to sound humorously scolding in spite of her exhaustion. "You and Lady Marie."

Christian smiled with his whole heart. He glanced over his shoulder at Marie, and his smile grew. "You're right, Mama," he said. "You need to regain your strength for the wedding."

A few more soft words were exchanged as Christian supervised the nurse tucking his mother in for a nap. He gave the order for the doctor to be called, only to find out a footman had already been sent to fetch him. There was nothing to do after that but to retreat downstairs.

"Do you need any other assistance here?" Ned asked, thumping Christian's shoulder in a brotherly manner.

"No," Christian breathed. He reached for Marie's hand, drawing her closer to his side. "I think we'll be all right."

Ned nodded, then exchanged a smile with Lady Aoife.

"Please do call on us if there is anything we can do," Lady Aoife said.

"We will," Marie answered for both herself and Christian.

A few more pleasantries were exchanged before Ned and Lady Aoife left. Once they were gone, Christian walked into the afternoon parlor with Marie. He wanted to flop into one of the chairs and let go of every ounce of tension he'd been holding for weeks. No, he wanted to go up to his bedroom and take Marie with him. Even if he didn't have the energy to make love to her, he would have been content just to hold her and sleep. Provided they were both naked, of course.

"I should go home, seeing as I'm such a mess," Marie said, attempting to pull her hand out of his.

He wouldn't let her go. Not only that, he tugged her closer, closing his arms around her and resting his forehead against hers.

"I love you and I want you, whether you're a mess or perfectly presentable," he said, then kissed her lips lightly. "I want you, whether you're wicked and scandalous or whether you're a saint. I want you in my life, in my arms, in my heart, and in my bed, from now until the end of time and beyond."

"You're in luck," she said, looping her arms over his shoulders and smiling. The heat in her eyes was enough to warm him for good. "Because I want you even more than you want me."

"Doubtful," he said, his heart swelling with affection and with peace.

"I could argue the point with you," Marie said, stealing a kiss. "And I probably will at some point."

"You won't win an argument about who loves who more," he said, laughing.

"Are you certain of that?" She arched one eyebrow.

"I'm certain that we'll have the rest of our lives to figure it out," he answered, then tightened his arms around her and kissed her until they were both breathless.

EPILOGUE

ONE YEAR LATER

Labor was easily the most miserable experience of Marie's life.

"I can't go on," she panted, then grunted as the urge to push overwhelmed her yet again.

"It won't be long now, my lady," the midwife said in a voice that was infuriatingly calm. "I can already see the head."

Marie wanted to tell the woman to hurry things along, but the best she could manage was a soul-shattering growl of pain as she pushed for all she was worth.

"Isn't there anything you can do to make the process easier?" Christian asked from the corner of the room, where he had been allowed to pace during Marie's delivery.

I KISSED AN EARL (AND I LIKE IT)

Everyone from the doctor—who had gotten himself thrown out of the room an hour before for irritating Marie—to the attending nurse had insisted men had no place at a birth, but Marie had absolutely refused to be parted from her husband.

"Babies come in their own time and in their own way, my lord," the midwife said in her soothing voice without looking at him.

Marie was too busy having her body split open to pay much mind to the exchange, but she did manage to shout, "Christian, come here this instant!"

Christian launched toward the bed, startling the nurse who stood ready with a receiving blanket beside a basin of water. "Yes, my darling?" he asked when he reached her side.

He made the mistake of swaying close enough to her that Marie was able to grab his arm as her pain reached an alarming crescendo. She squeezed so hard that Christian cried out as well, half crumpling on the bed.

"This is your doing," Marie ground out, even as most of her effort went into bringing the baby into the world. "You and your naked."

She wasn't certain if she'd spoken a coherent thought or not, but Christian seemed to accept his part in the whole thing. "I know, I know," he gasped, "and I'm sorry. But I won't promise not to do it again."

Marie cried out—partly in pain, partly because she could feel the moment had come as the midwife cooed soothingly and reached between her legs, and partly because she wanted to laugh at Christian's off-color comment but couldn't.

"Here we go, my lady, here we go," the midwife called out, an excited look in her eyes.

The moment was horrible, wonderful, unbelievable, and indescribable, but within seconds, Marie felt as though she'd been turned inside out, physically and emotionally, as a tiny cry rent the air.

"Here she is, my lady," the midwife said in a delighted voice. She nodded for the nurse to come forward with some sort of clamp and scissors.

All of the pain, all of the stress and misery were forgotten entirely the moment the midwife lifted the mottled, bloody, and squalling baby girl to show Marie.

"It's a baby," Christian gasped, astonishment and bliss lighting his expression. "You actually had a baby."

"We did," Marie corrected him. She reached for the tiny girl as the midwife handed her over, then began the afterbirth clean-up. Marie wanted to laugh and cry and gasp in wonder as she held her daughter for the first time.

"You did all the work," Christian said, laughing and weeping with her as he sank onto the bed, sliding his arm around Marie to support her.

She needed the support as well. Labor had only lasted seven hours, but she was more exhausted than she'd ever been in her life. She was also more in love than she'd ever been, with both her daughter and Christian. She leaned her head against his chest, closing her eyes for a moment and counting her blessings over how lucky she was.

"She appears to be fine and healthy," the midwife said as she and the nurse took care of the aftermath. A wry grin lit the woman's face. "Perhaps a little too healthy, if you'll forgive my impertinence. No one is going to believe that darling girl is three months early."

Marie knew she should be embarrassed by giving birth six months after her wedding to Christian. In truth, it could have been worse. They'd caused enough of a scandal by marrying only six months after the deaths of Christian's father and brother. Even by modern standards, it hadn't been enough time for proper mourning. But everyone in County Antrim was already whispering about the need for such scandalous haste. Those whispers had grown in volume when Marie began to show within two months of the wedding. It was exactly the sort of thing society expected from one of those wicked O'Shea sisters.

Neither Marie nor Christian cared one whit, though.

"I can't stop staring at her," Christian said, his voice tight with emotion. He nestled closer to Marie, reaching around to stroke their daughter's head. "And to think that something so alive and miraculous could come hard on the heels of such tragedy."

"The natural successor to death is life," Marie reasoned. "Just as the natural progression after sorrow is joy."

"Joy," Christian repeated, resting his cheek against the top of Marie's head. "What do you think of that for a name?"

Marie's heart flipped excitedly. "I think that would be perfect," she said. She beamed down at their daughter. "Welcome to the world, Joy."

"May you bring as much happiness and excitement to this world as your dear mama has brought to me," Christian added, brushing his thumb over little Joy's brow, then kissing Marie's cheek. "Though you're as likely as not to bring chaos, mischief, and trouble to the world as anything else. Just like your mama."

Marie laughed. "Just like your papa, you mean," she corrected him.

"Just like the both of us," Christian said, settling the matter.

Marie glanced up at him, meeting his grin with one of her own. She couldn't imagine her life being any more perfect than it was with Christian and their family.

I HOPE YOU ENJOYED MARIE AND CHRISTIAN'S story! They were such fun characters to write. And so are the rest of the O'Shea sisters! Like Colleen. Gosh, she really hates Lord Boleran. She finds him boorish, arrogant, and overbearing. Or does she just think those things to hide an entirely different set of feelings she has for him? What happens when a mystery causes her to go snooping on his property in the middle of the night? And will Colleen be able to survive the scandal of being caught? Find out in *If You Wannabe My Marquess*. Keep clicking to get started reading Chapter One!

If you enjoyed this book and would like to hear more from me, please sign up for my newsletter! When you sign up, you'll get a free, full-length novella, *A Passionate Deception*. Victorian identity theft has never been so exciting in this story of hope, tricks, and starting over. Part of my West Meets East series, *A Passionate Deception* can be read as a stand-alone. Pick up your free copy today by signing up to receive my newsletter (which I only send out when I have a new release)!

Sign up here: http://eepurl.com/cbaVMH

Are you on social media? I am! Come and join the fun on Facebook: http://www.facebook.com/merryfarmerreaders

I'm also a huge fan of Instagram and post lots of original content there: https://www.instagram.com/merryfarmer/

. . .

AND NOW, GET STARTED ON IF YOU WANNABE MY MARQUESS...

BALLYMENA, IRELAND – SEPTEMBER, 1888

IT WAS A SIMPLE FACT OF NATURE THAT MEN considered it their purpose in life to dominate and manage women. Colleen O'Shea had seen the nefarious intentions of the male of the species play out over and over. She'd see it in the way the schoolmaster who had been hired to serve as tutor for her brother, Lord Fergus O'Shea, Earl of Ballymena, had fawned over Fergus and snubbed her and her sisters when all they'd wanted to do was learn. She'd noted it when the great lords of County Antrim had looked down their noses at the fine, intelligent ladies they asked to dance at balls and soirees, as if all the ladies had to offer were shapely bosoms instead of bright minds. And she noticed it in the way Fergus had declared his intention to bully and badger all of his sisters into marriage, now that he'd returned to Ireland. He'd already managed to catch Colleen's sister, Marie, in his marriage trap—although, to be honest, Marie hadn't put up much of a fight. That had more to do with her new husband, Lord Christian Darrow, Earl of Kilrea, and his handsome face and teasing eyes, than convincing Fergus might have done.

Colleen, however, was determined to fight her brother's meddling and the institution of marriage tooth and nail. She had no intention of falling victim to the domination that so many men still thought they were entitled to. Hadn't they read the exciting works of the progressive women who were heralding a new age of female independence? Had they never heard of the lines of Annie Besant, Emmeline Pankhurst, or Harriet McIlquham?

Fergus most likely thought his heart was in the right place as he scoured northern Ireland for men to marry his womenfolk, but as Colleen and her sisters well knew, he had committed one major mistake while attempting to appease them. In exchange for curtailing their freedom by forcing them to move from the seaside cottage, where the four of them had been residing, back into the main house of Dunegard Castle, he had given them all bicycles of the highest quality and most modern design. Said bicycles enabled the sisters to embrace their freedom rather than curtailing it.

"Are you certain it was a good idea to strap barrels of beer to the back of these things?" Colleen panted, peddling the last few yards through the back alley behind Ballymena's main street. She'd long since broken out in a sweat, and she was reasonably certain her legs wouldn't support her once they stopped in back of The Hangman Pub and dismounted to deliver their order.

"This is the perfect solution to our transportation problems," Shannon—Colleen's oldest sister—said, out of breath herself. "Since Fergus forbid us to use the cart."

"Which one of you alerted him to our ongoing

commercial activities?" Marie huffed, straining to pedal the last bit of the journey to the pub.

Ahead, in the alley, Mr. Coney, the pub's owner, had stepped out of the pub and was watching the four sisters struggle forward with their loads. He wore a grin that Colleen found far too indulgent for her tastes.

"It wasn't me," Chloe—her youngest sister—said in a hurry. Chloe's face was red from exertion, and her ginger hair was plastered to her forehead with sweat.

It was likely that all four of them looked more like exhausted farmhands and not the titled ladies they were. If anyone had seen the sisters of an earl loitering in the alley in back of a common pub, puffing from the effort of riding bicycles laden with barrels of beer, none of them would have withstood the scandal, regardless of what advances the likes of Emmeline Pankhurst was making for their sex.

Shannon shot a wary look to Chloe. "Perhaps it would be best if we pretended our brewing venture no longer existed at all," she said with a narrow-eyed look.

"But women have been brewers for centuries," Chloe protested as they rode up to The Hangman's back door. "It was an exclusively female endeavor all through the Middle Ages. I read about it in a History book. The book didn't even have pictures."

Marie laughed as she shifted her feet from her bicycle's pedals to the ground and leaned forward over her handlebars. "Is it only books without pictures that have authority, then?" she asked.

I KISSED AN EARL (AND I LIKE IT)

"I'd be surprised if you've read a book at all recently," Colleen teased her with a lopsided grin. "I'm surprised you deigned to leave your dear, delicious husband for more than a few minutes to join us."

"Christian believes it is important for a woman to have her own interests and activities, even when she is married," Marie said with a mock imperious look. She couldn't hold the look, though, and dissolved into wicked giggles. "Besides, he's a bit sore today."

Shannon rolled her eyes. Chloe blinked obliviously. Colleen knew enough to guess that Marie was talking about sexual relations, but it was beyond her why Lord Kilrea would be sore. From the gossip she'd heard, it was the lady who was far more likely to end up smarting as a result of the marriage bed.

"I'm surprised that Lord Kilrea let you out of the house at all," Colleen said, dismounting her bicycle with a groan. Fortunately, a young man from the pub joined Mr. Coney in unstrapping the barrels of beer and taking them into the pub so she didn't have to exert herself further. "I'm surprise you're able to have your own thoughts at all, seeing as you were so foolish as to fall into Fergus's marriage trap."

"Yes, Marie," Chloe added with a scolding click of her tongue. "That really was unwise of you."

"I believe our dear sister feels she's made a good bargain in trading her freedom for *other things*," Shannon said, sending Marie a downright wicked look.

Marie met that look with a teasing flicker of one

eyebrow. "There are benefits to finding oneself under a man."

Colleen was certain she was speaking in some sort of double entendre, but she ignored what she didn't fully understand and shook her head. "You'll never catch me tripping up to the point where Fergus arranges a marriage just to stop a scandal."

"You may find yourself agreeing to Fergus's marital dealings for other reasons," Marie warned her with a sly look.

"Who, Colleen?" Chloe snorted. "Never."

"You ladies look as though you've been rode hard and put up wet," Mr. Coney said once all four barrels had been taken from their bicycles into the pub. "I know it ain't proper for the likes of you to patronize my pub, but if you'd care to come inside and sit a while, I'll have Maeve make you some tea."

"A sampling of some of your weaker ale would be good enough for us," Shannon said, looking more like a fishwife than the eldest sister of an earl as she wiped her hands on her skirt and followed Mr. Coney into the pub. "We need to talk about the price of this shipment anyhow."

Colleen was more than happy to leave the business dealings of their brewing enterprise to Shannon. Shannon was the one with the head for business anyhow. Colleen fancied herself the sister with the finest palate and routinely adjusted the recipe for their beer. She had

I KISSED AN EARL (AND I LIKE IT)

no qualms at all—even though she knew she should—striding into the backroom of the pub and following Mr. Coney's handsome young assistant as he directed her to a table near the door that led into the main part of the pub. She accepted a half-pint of ale and settled in to enjoy it, Marie and Chloe sitting at the small table beside her.

That was when she heard two familiar voices speaking low on the other side of the doorway.

"I need you to keep the dragon for me, Benedict." The man speaking had to be their cousin, Cailean O'Shea, Viscount Dervock. Colleen would know his melodious voice anywhere.

"Of course, I'll keep it." The reply came from Lord Benedict Boleran. Just the idea that Lord Boleran was in the next room, probably looking all smug and handsome —no, that wasn't the word she wanted to describe him— smug and *haughty*, had Colleen's temperature rising higher than it already was. She could feel her cheeks burning.

"Lord Boleran," Chloe whispered, then clapped a hand over her mouth and dissolved into giggles.

"Oh, dear." Marie rolled her eyes, her mouth tugging into a lopsided smile. She shook her head at Colleen.

"What are those reactions for?" Colleen hissed. "You know I simply cannot abide Lord Boleran."

"Oh, yes. You simply *cannot abide* him." Marie mocked her.

Colleen made a sound of disgust, even as she pressed

a hand to her stomach. The ale she'd been served was stronger than she'd thought it would be, that must be it. Because there was no one in Ireland or beyond whom she hated more than Lord Boleran. Every time she'd encountered him, the man was stiff, morose, insufferable, and gorgeous.

No, that wasn't the word she was searching for either. Lord Boleran condescended to her in the worst possible way. He'd barely tolerated her visit several weeks ago, after Lord Kilrea's father and brother were killed in that unfortunate carriage accident, when Marie had implored her to ask Lord Boleran what he had observed about the wrecked carriage. He seemed to disapprove of her every time their paths crossed in town or at a ball. And yet, he always made it a point to torture her with an invitation to dance or a passing hello when she did not wish to speak to him.

Colleen's sisters continued to stare at her as if they knew something she didn't. She shook her head and deliberately ignored them, leaning toward the doorway to listen in on Lord Boleran and Cousin Cailean's conversation.

"...too big to put anywhere else," Cailean was saying. "And the poor thing requires such careful care and feeding, if you'll pardon the expression."

"Perfectly apt," Lord Boleran said.

"And what with my recent land sale...." Cailean let out a sigh. Colleen didn't need to hear him explain. They all knew that Cailean was strapped for cash and that he had resorted to selling off parts of his estate to pay his debtors. "The dragon will be better off in your care, for the time being," Cailean went on. "I trust you to keep it safe."

"The dragon?" Chloe whispered.

Colleen shrugged. She'd never heard of such a thing. At least, not outside of the world of fantasy.

"Your dragon will be welcome on my land," Lord Boleran said. "Provided it doesn't breathe fire and burn my barn down."

The two men laughed. Colleen was more confused than ever. Cailean was known to be eccentric, but if Lord Boleran was intent on indulging his fantasies...well, that was simply cruel.

"If you will excuse me for a moment," Cailean said. Colleen heard the sound of him getting up and moving away from the table.

Silence followed, which suggested Lord Boleran was seated at the table alone.

"I'm going to get to the bottom of this," Colleen whispered to her sisters.

Before either of them could stop her, she got up, brushed her hair back from her face, squared her shoulders, and marched through the canvas curtain separating the back of the pub from the front.

WANT TO READ MORE?
PICK UP IF YOU WANNABE MY MARQUESS TODAY!

Click here for a complete list of other works by Merry Farmer.

ABOUT THE AUTHOR

I hope you have enjoyed *I Kissed an Earl* (*and I Liked It*). If you'd like to be the first to learn about when new books in the series come out and more, please sign up for my newsletter here: http://eepurl.com/cbaVMH And remember, Read it, Review it, Share it! For a complete list of works by Merry Farmer with links, please visit http://wp.me/P5ttjb-14F.

Merry Farmer is an award-winning novelist who lives in suburban Philadelphia with her cats, Torpedo, her grumpy old man, and Justine, her hyperactive new baby. She has been writing since she was ten years old and realized one day that she didn't have to wait for the teacher to assign a creative writing project to write something. It was the best day of her life. She then went on to earn not one but two degrees in History so that she would always have something to write about. Her books have reached the Top 100 at Amazon, iBooks, and Barnes & Noble, and have been named finalists in the prestigious RONE and Rom Com Reader's Crown awards.

ACKNOWLEDGMENTS

I owe a huge debt of gratitude to my awesome beta-readers, Caroline Lee and Jolene Stewart, for their suggestions and advice. And double thanks to Julie Tague, for being a truly excellent editor and to Cindy Jackson for being an awesome assistant!

Click here for a complete list of other works by Merry Farmer.

Made in the USA
Monee, IL
04 October 2021